October '87.

ROBBIE

If you enjoy this book
you would probably enjoy our other Kelpies.

Here's a complete list to choose from:

CATCH A KELPIE

for further details of Canongate Kelpies write to
Canongate Publishing, 17 Jeffrey Street, Edinburgh

ROBBIE

Emil Pacholek

CANONGATE · KELPIES

First published 1980 by Andre Deutsch Ltd
First published in Kelpies 1986

copyright © 1980 Emil Pacholek

Cover illustration by Jill Downie

Printed in Great Britain
by Cox & Wyman Ltd, Reading, Berkshire

ISBN 0 86241 113 0

*The publisher acknowledges subsidy
of the Scottish Arts Council
towards the publication of this volume.*

for Norma and Ben

CANONGATE PUBLISHING LTD
17 JEFFREY STREET, EDINBURGH EH1 1DR

CONTENTS

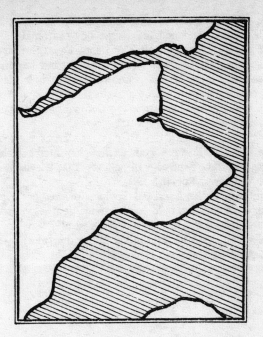

ON THE EAST COAST of Scotland, between the Firths of Tay
and Forth, there lies Fife, shaped like the head of a dog,
looking out, ears pricked and alert, over the North Sea.

If an eye were to be added to the outline, it would be placed
just below the rip of the Eden Estuary. And it is there that
we find the village of Kincaple.

It was there, in this farm village, in days of changing from
old ways to new, that Robbie grew up . . .

'It was fantastic, Grandfather! Just fantastic!'

Robbie's eyes were saucer-wide with excitement as the
words fair bubbled from him.

'The whole class was there, in Kenny Kaye's house — they've
got television, you know! A set in their own living-room! And
we all saw it — the Queen and the horses and the soldiers and the
coaches and the crown with a diamond as big as a hen's egg!'

The old man sat into the cushions on the chair at the fireside, smiling and nodding as the boy chattered on.

'I'm going to get pally with that Kenny Kaye, give him some conkers this year or some marbles maybe, and he might let me see some more! It was fantastic – the whole class was there and Ferret Ferrier got a skelp for nipping one of the lassies – but it was fantastic! The Coronation and that – we saw it all!'

'Television, eh?' said the old man, poking at the red glow in the fireplace. It was a summer fire, low in the grate, just keeping a kettle on the edge of boiling. 'That television stuff'll go for your eyes, Robbie.'

'But, Grandfather,' insisted Robbie, 'the teacher said that someday everybody would have a television!'

The old man smiled and shook his head.

'Television? No, Robbie, folk'll no' bother much with the thing. All that starin' in the dark.'

THE JACKDAW TREE

THERE WAS NO SIGN of the village of Kincaple from the main road. It lay hidden behind a roll of hills and a dense tangle of trees, a secret from the world, except in winter time, when long trails of goose-grey woodsmoke gave it away.

The houses that huddled in the village were of sandstone, low, pantile-roofed cottages, some standing on their own, others in rows of threes or fours – and all cradled in the arms of Kincaple Wood.

They were the homes of the farm workers, the horsemen, the orramen, the tractormen.

The cottage Robbie lived in was on its own, and the one that stood nearest to the fringe of the trees.

So near in fact, that when there was a wind in the wood, Robbie could lie in bed at night and listen to the rush of the leaves and the creak of branches as they rubbed one against the other.

One night, as he lay close to sleeping, Robbie heard a roar, like a lion's roar, but by the time he scrambled over to the window and peered out into the silver moonlight, there was no sign.

But he was sure that it had been a lion, and a pretty big one at that . . .

When morning came, Robbie ran round to the green door in the row of cottages round the corner, next to the washhouse where his mother was already steeping the wash in the great fat, black boiler.

Inside the cottage, his grandfather was standing by the fender, painting his chin with soap from a mug on the mantelpiece. The old man listened calmly, taking it all in, and nodding every now and then.

And when Robbie asked if it could have been a lion that he'd heard in the night, the old man didn't scoff or dismiss it. Instead, he thought for a while, scraping the open razor down the stretched side of his face, frowning, weighing things up.

Then he said it might have been, although he'd heard that all the lions had gone away a while back.

He wiped the lather from the blade, then stropped it on a blackened leather belt.

But the best thing to do, he thought, was to go and see for themselves.

And they did.

Robbie took a stick just in case, and the pair of them went off in search, tramping through the ferns and the bracken and the tall clumps of thunderflower.

They saw rabbits and squirrels and a hare and a hedgehog or two. And once, briefly, they saw a roe deer rise up and glide out of some long grass and away.

But they never saw a lion.

Kincaple Wood was a magical place, full of wonder and adventure and enchantment.

A place that, on long summer evenings, fairly rattled and rang with laughter.

The whole village, all the workers from the farm and their wives and their bairns used to gather there. The same men only hours before had been racked and soaked in the sweat of their labours – but now they were free and ran and capered and charged like young horses slipped of their bridles.

It was hide-and-seek, with bodies coiled like snakes on low branches, hiding, hiding, hiding – then all leaping down and racing through the trees and back to the base near the old doocot!

Even the old man! And Robbie, too, laughing well into the night until all the shadows merged into one, and the chill of evening came down about them.

Kincaple Wood was a magical place.

10

Robbie and the old man loved the wood, and already Robbie was able to tell all the different trees by name – by the buds and the leaves, and by the bark, sometimes as smooth as skin as with the beech, and sometimes like the weathered, winter furrows on a ploughed field, as with the oaks and the elms.

And within the wood were the special trees. Like the huge horse chestnut that in summer fairly frothed with blossom, then yielded majestic conkers that, when strung on a bootlace, were more than a match for any others in the school playground.

Then there was the conifer with the spongey bark that Robbie could punch just as hard as he liked and never once hurt his knuckles!

And the elm, with the long, low branch like a dragon's tail that he could hang upside-down on or swing on or ride like a wild horse until it was tamed.

But there was one tree that was extra. One tree that was special above all the rest.

It was known simply as the Jackdaw Tree.

It was old and crooked and had grown with a great twist through it like some huge hand had been turning it into the ground, and over the years it had been nested in by hundreds and thousands of jackdaws. Pile upon pile, nest upon nest, storey upon storey, until it was a solid platform of twigs.

When Robbie climbed it for the first time, it was the most exciting thing he'd ever done, and he could hardly move for the tremble running through him. It must have been like that for Hillary and Tensing on the roof of the world he'd thought and for the whole of that day, he'd sat high in the branches watching the life all around him.

The eggs, a pale, sort of forgotten shade of blue, were speckled with black, and were laid in nests lined with rags and scraps of paper and bits of binder twine and wisps of sheep's wool that had been teased off on the hawthorn hedges that skirted the fields.

And when the young jackdaws were hatched, the sky all around was flecked like the eggs with scores of parent birds, fetching and carrying food to cram down the gaping beaks.

11

Then last year, on the ground beneath the tree, hiding in at the very roots, Robbie had found the young bird. It had fallen from a nest, and its wing had been twisted.

Robbie had carried it home in his jersey and the old man had helped him feed it. At first, the bird had turned its head away from the bread soaked in milk and the boy had to prise its beak open and let the liquid trickle down the jackdaw's throat. It took only an instant for the bird to make up its mind that it was a taste to be enjoyed, and soon it was a non-stop job for Robbie and his grandfather to keep up with the jackdaw's cackling demands.

It grew quickly, beautifully black with a smoke-grey head that it cocked to the side when Robbie spoke to it.

The jackdaw used to perch on the boy's shoulder, then flutter clumsily to the old man, and more than once it knocked the pipe from his mouth in an explosion of ash and panic as it clawed and fluttered its way up to his shoulder.

It was a fine bird, a bonnie bird, but it never was able to fly and one day, when Robbie was at school, as it perched on a spade handle, it was snatched by the Cunninghams' cat.

The old man heard the clacking and rushed from his house waving his stick and shouting — but too late.

He picked up all the feathers and buried them deep and when Robbie came off the bus at night, the old man met him and said that, as if by some miracle, the bird's wing had suddenly clicked into place and it had taken to flying and had circled the cottage a couple of times and then gone.

Robbie waited a long, long time for the bird to come back, but it never did — although he was sure he saw it once or twice, cocking its head to the side as he spoke, high in the branches of the Jackdaw Tree.

Time in Kincaple Wood, like in any other wood, was not measured in days, or weeks, or months, but in changes, in seasons, each one blending with the other yet each one so very different.

Summer, when the wood was full and fat and green.

And Autumn, when all was losing colour, drawing pale and dry and brittle.

And then Winter, when you could see far into the wood and even to the grey daylight at the other side in places. When the whole countryside was bleak and cold and hard as slate.

But Spring was never far away, and it was Spring that Robbie and the old man loved the best.

Spring, when the daffodils were up and nodding and golden. And leaves had newly burst in a great green explosion, and young birds were edging out along the branches into them.

It was in Springtime that they met the man.

They had been walking in the wood together, Robbie and the old man, when they came across him.

He came out of a pick-up van, reached into the back of it and picked up a brush and a pot of white paint.

The old man and the boy watched, puzzled, as the figure made his way through the wood. Every now and then he stopped then daubed a bold white cross on the trunk of a tree.

Robbie's heart gave a lurch as he saw the man pause at the Jackdaw Tree.

'Fine day, though,' said the old man, casual like, when they were beside him.

'What's that you're doing?' asked Robbie.

'Contract,' came the short reply. 'Timber felling contract.'

Robbie looked high above him, to a clutter of young jackdaws that were holding out their ragged wings to the breeze.

'When's this?' The words tore at Robbie's dried throat.

'The weekend.'

The man dipped his brush into the paint, slapped the surplus from it, and right in front of Robbie and the old man, he painted a stark cross on the trunk of the Jackdaw Tree!

'But you'll no' get much in the way of good timber out of this old tree,' said Robbie's grandfather, puzzled.

'That's right,' nodded the timber contractor.

'Then – then why chop it down?' asked Robbie.

The man jerked his head towards a big oak.

'That's the fellow we're after, but this one's in the road. Still, it'll be fine for firewood.'

13

'But – but, the jackdaws!' exclaimed the boy. 'The tree's full of young birds! What about all of them?'

The man shrugged, then ruffled Robbie's hair. 'Can't be helped, son,' was all he said.

The confusion flapped in the boy.

'But can you not wait? Even a month or so?'

The timber contractor fished in his top pocket with his finger and thumb, then drew out a notebook. He flicked through the pages.

'I'm here at Kincaple today,' he said. 'Then it's up to Perth the morn. Then down to near Kirkcaldy. I mark the trees, and a couple of days later, there's two cutters following behind me.'

He shook his head.

'If they didn't get this lot down by this weekend, it could be months afore they're back this way again.' He grinned at Robbie. 'And time's money in this game, son. Pounds, shillings and pence – that's what it's a' about.'

With no more than that he was gone, pausing for only a second as he slapped a white cross onto the bark of the great oak tree behind them.

For long moments, the old man and the boy watched. No words were spoken, none were needed. They just stood and looked at the tears of paint that trickled down through the furrows of the bark.

Above them, young jackdaws cackled and cawed and took little, dare-devil hops into the air. Almost away . . . almost . . .

The two days that lay before the weekend were long drawn-out affairs.

On the Thursday night, Robbie sat in with the old man, closer and closer to crying.

'It's just not right, is it?' He must have said it a hundred times.

And the old man placed his hand lightly on the boy's shoulders, hurt and angry about what was surely going to happen, and sickened further by the fact that he had nothing in him that could comfort the boy.

'Life's a cruel-like thing at times, Robbie,' he tried, but it was no use. The words were like chaff.

The old man crossed the room to the table that stood at the side of the fireplace. He turned on the wireless.

'We might pick up the trawlermen,' he said brightly, waiting for the set to warm up. But when he twirled at the tuning knob, all he got were squeaks and buzzes and crackles and whistles.

'Needs a new accumulator, I doubt,' sighed the old man, switching the set off.

'Here, did I ever tell you about my grand-dad and the night the Tay Bridge fell down?' the grandfather tried again.

Robbie had heard the tale many times of how the old man's grandfather had just missed the train at Leuchars – then the thing had gone off the bridge and into the swirling black waters of the Tay – and although the boy usually loved the tale and its telling, this time was different, somehow.

'Aye, you told me,' he said quietly.

Then with a sigh, the boy got up.

'I'll see you tomorrow, then,' was all he said as he drew the door onto its catch and left.

And the next night was the same. Except worse, for late on they heard the chug and rattle of the woodcutter's van as it arrived, passing close by the old man's cottage on its way up the track into the wood.

'Maybe if I talked to them?' Robbie suggested, but the old man shook his head.

'But if they could only wait,' went on the boy. 'Even a month, or a couple of weeks until all the young are flown . . .'

The old man sighed.

'They've got their job to do, I suppose,' he said.

And then, simply, seeing that it was hopeless, the boy gave in to crying, his body shuddering as he huddled in close to the old man.

Robbie's grandfather held him tight, shaking his head, shaking, shaking, and after the boy had left for home he still sat by his fireside for a long, long while . . .

Saturday came as Saturday had to, and Robbie rose to face the day he'd been dreading.

As he'd lain awake for long hours in the night, he decided that all he could do was to be there when it happened, and to try to save as many of the birds as he could. In the morning, he gathered together some big boxes, and an old rabbit hutch and a wooden barrel – anything at all to keep the young jackdaws in.

Then, with a dull, heavy feeling in his body, he swung over the stile at the fence and into the wood.

The woodcutters, two of them, had parked their van in a clearing.

As Robbie approached, he saw that one had an axe, and the other a long saw arced across his shoulder.

But they weren't cutting trees. And they weren't about to either.

They were simply scratching at their heads and pointing. There! And there and there and there!

And all around them! For on every single tree was painted a bold, white cross!

And there was not a thing in the world that the men could do! Every tree was marked – every oak, every elm, every single tree. The woodcutters just didn't know which trees to cut and which to leave!

Robbie raced like a hare through the wood! The Jackdaw Tree! The Jackdaw Tree had been saved!

He vaulted the fence and dashed to the old man's cottage. 'Grandfather! Grandfather!' he yelled, hammering on the door. 'The men – they don't know which trees to cut down! They've all got crosses on!'

But there was no reply.

The old man wasn't in his cottage. He was in the wash-house.

He was rubbing at a pair of trousers on the zinc scrubbing board. Trying to get rid of some splashes of white paint.

THE GOLF

ON THE SATURDAY MORNING before the start of the Open Championship in July, 1955, Robbie pedalled the three miles from Kincaple to the links at St Andrews to see the great golfers practise.

The wind was from the West and strong, sweeping him along, and the tyres of his bike fairly swished on the road still wet from the overnight rain.

As his legs pedalled, his heart hammered, and as his heart hammered, his head raced with his plan.

All the great golfers were there, all chasing the trophy and the fantastic cheque of one thousand pounds!

Robbie, in turn, was chasing them.

He watched them all day, following them round the Old Course, tagging along with the crowds, all the way out along the links to the Eden Estuary where he could just make out the shape of Kincaple Woods in the mirk, then round the loop and back towards the grey, cathedral city of St Andrews.

Even when the wind dropped and the rain came and the spectators thinned out and straggled for home, Robbie stayed on, waiting for the moment to be right.

Like when Peter Thomson put his tee-shot right in close at the short eighth. Or when Bobby Locke exploded the ball up and out of the wet, clinging sand in Hell Bunker. Or when the great Byron Nelson of America took his time to line up a long putt on the tricky green at the Road Hole, then sent the ball straight into the back of the cup. These were the moments Robbie chose.

With each golfer it was the same story.

'Excuse me, Mister,' he said. 'You're playing some grand-like golf – do you think you could sign one of your golf balls

17

for me. It would be a fine thing having one wi' the winner's name on it . . .'

Put that way, it was a request none could refuse, particularly when it came from a drookit wee figure with his hair slicked down with the rain.

When Robbie cycled home at tea-time he was soaked through to the skin – but he had a dozen golf balls in his pockets, each and every one signed by a great player. It was raw cold on his bike and his trousers rubbed red on his legs, but he wobbled home into the wind triumphant. With a bit of luck one of the golf balls would have the winner's name on it . . .

On the Friday the Championship was over. To Robbie's delight, last year's winner, Peter Thomson, had done it again – and he was one of the players who'd signed.

On a newspaper in his room, Robbie painted an egg-cup silver, and when it was dry he placed the ball in it. It took pride of place, right in the middle of his mantelpiece.

The other golf balls were taken out into the wash-house and, in a pailful of hot, soapy Rinso, were scrubbed clean.

Robbie sold them to the grocer's van for tenpence each.

THE TRACTION
ENGINE

IT WAS HARVEST TIME, and the field between the Kincaple road and the old Seafields Brickworks was almost gone.

A pair of clattering binders had cut at it strip by strip until there was just a narrow band of oats left. Another half dozen sweeps maybe and it would be done.

Since early that morning, Robbie had been out helping, picking up the sheaves one under each arm after they had been cut and bound and cast out from the binder, then leaning them together like old friends whispering, to dry out in stooks in the warmth of the late August sun.

Robbie looked across at the last of the oats, the last field of the last crop. Then he turned his gaze up the road, to where it curled round behind the trees into the village of Kincaple itself.

There was still no sign of the old man.

If he didn't hurry, he'd be too late. There could only be about four more runs left and it would be all over.

But then, at that very moment, he was there! The old man, whose eyes were as blue and as clear and as strong as they had always been, although his body was now ageing and needed the stick to support it.

He saw Robbie's arm arc in the air and lengthened his stride, hurrying as much as he was able.

'I thought you were going to miss the end, Grandfather,' said Robbie when they were together.

The old man smiled.

'No . . . I was . . . em, held up,' he said, remembering how soft the chair had been at his door, and how warm the sun on his face, and how his afternoon nap had lasted longer than he'd meant it to.

'Come on, though,' he urged, ruffling at the boy's hair. 'The binders are coming!'

At the top of the field, by the old brickworks fence, the tractors swung round and began to tow the reapers on their final runs.

Down and down they came, with the blades of the binders turning, turning, turning, flashing in the sunlight, sweeping the last of the oats onto the chattering cutters and away.

The old man stood silently, watching them lurch past in front of him. His mind was miles away as he watched the tall, ripe harvest fall, and for a moment the rattle of the binder became something else as he day-dreamed of men, and trenches and fields red with poppies long ago.

Then, strangely, he took the cap from his head as if in respect of an old friend's passing, and put his hand on the boy's shoulder.

'Well, that's another year,' he said softly, when the binders had stopped at the foot of the run. 'And not a rabbit in sight, poor things . . .'

It had been the first harvest without them, that autumn of '55. Up until that year, the fields had moved with rabbits, and at the end of the cutting, the men used to gather round, watching as the crop shook and swayed in runs as the rabbits shoaled closer and closer together, driven by the noise and the smell and the fear.

Then, at the very last of it, they'd all rushed out in two's and three's and four's, scattering across the stubble, like water spilled on a stove.

Most got away, but some didn't – and there was not a cottage in the village that didn't have the sweet aroma of rabbit stew wafting through it.

At the time, Robbie – and the old man, too – had felt a sadness for the ones that were caught and had smiled for the ones that had bobtailed over the sheaves and away.

But it had not been freedom they'd been escaping to last year. It had been the blindness, and the trembling, and the

20

misery, and the end of nearly every single rabbit in the countryside.

'I never thought I'd miss them so much,' the old man said. 'But I do, for all that.'

Robbie nodded. Then he tugged at the sleeve of his grandfather's jacket.

'Come on, though – I've got something to show you.'

He led the old man through the stooks, down towards the endriggs of the field, near to the ash trees that lined the Kincaple road.

And there they stopped.

'What do you think?' asked Robbie, eager for the old man's judgement.

In the shade of one of the ash trees, were three tiny stacks – round and even and full, straight-sided, perfect in miniature.

Instead of joining the men for the afternoon piece-break, Robbie had taken just a quick swig of the cool, oatmeal drink from the pitcher, then had gone off on his own.

He'd gathered together some handfuls of stubble, selecting them carefully for evenness of length. Then he'd placed them in a circle, with the clods of red, clay earth meeting at the centre.

Round and round he'd laid the courses, piling the stack until it was about a foot high. After he'd tapered it to a point and thatched the top with straw, the job was complete.

A tiny, perfect copy of a stackyard.

'Aye,' nodded his grandfather, who'd shown Robbie how to do it. 'We'd better hae a word with the grieve – you're just about ready for the real thing!'

They laughed together, and then it was home, with the stubble crunching like frosted snow beneath their boots.

At the top of the field, near to where it met the first trees of Kincaple Wood, the old man and the boy stopped to rest and gazed down behind them.

The land fell away in a long, gentle sweep down and down towards the Eden estuary. The tide was almost full in, a high Lammas tide, and the breeze from its shores was cool and welcome.

The pair of them stood for a while, feeling its soft touch upon their faces, and just gazing at the land they loved so much.

The binders were leaving now, swaying and lurching through the rutted gateway in the hawthorn hedging. Following the two tractors, a single Clydesdale was pulling a flat wagon, and the men sat round the edges of it, dangling their weary legs over the sides, laughing, joking, glad that the last field of the last crop was all cut.

It was fine weather, and the wind was light and from the west, so with luck, it would hold and the stacking would be quick and easy when the oats were right dried.

After the men had gone and there was no more clatter and rattle and creaking from the wagon, a feeling of peace and tranquillity settled like a picnic blanket over the countryside.

A bird began to sing from a high tree behind them, and when the song was repeated, they both knew that it was a mavis.

Then a scattering of wood pigeons flew out, circled over and flopped down among the stooks to fill their crops, pecking and bobbing round in little circles like clockwork toys.

As Robbie and his grandfather gazed down at the neat lines in front of them, the old man gave a quick smile, and when the boy asked him why, he shook his head.

'I was just thinking,' he said, dreaming again, 'how much it's all changed. None of your new-fangled tractors and binders when I was a laddie – it was all horse we had. And we had to bind the sheaves ourselves, bunching them and then tying them tight with a twist of their own straw. From first light till last, with only the Sabbath off to ourselves – and even then, just sometimes . . .'

Robbie's grandfather looked a long way away.

'Aye,' he added suddenly as he came back. 'But it's a sorry-like harvest without the rabbits. I never thought I'd miss them, but I do for all that.'

And they turned their backs and went home.

22

Although the next day was to end in a most unexpected manner, it began just as Robbie knew it would.

Every day had the same beginnings.

The pig was fed first. Robbie had scarcely started to tip the mash of boiled potatoes and scraps and meal into the trough, when it came rushing out of the sty, skidding and slithering on the concrete floor, squealing with delight and excitement. It burrowed its snout into the food, snapping, snorting and slurping the stuff down just as fast as it was able.

'It's coming on fine!' cried Robbie, rubbing his hand along the length of the long, pink flank, feeling the wiry hairs tickle across his palm.

The old man nodded.

'Aye, maybe a month yet and we'll get him taken through to the mart in Cupar – if he doesn't choke himself between times!'

Then a couple of scoops of corn were fed to the hens in the run behind the sty. That day, the seven hens had given six eggs, and one bird was still sitting. It was a fine start to the day.

Robbie's grandfather looked up into the sky, licked a forefinger and held it aloft.

'Well, Robbie – and what do you think? A walk, maybe?'

There was no maybe about it – a walk it was. Robbie had no idea why the old man went through the ritual of inspecting the sky and testing the wind, for they went their walks regardless.

They had gone in rain when Robbie's mother had shaken her head and sighed as she'd watched them leave from behind a beaded curtain of raindrops at the doorway.

And they had gone when the wind had been tearing at the trees all around the village and the long grass on the bankings at the sides of the roads had rolled and swelled like heavy seas.

But this day, there was scarcely enough wind to show the light side of a leaf, and the sky was clear and high and already a lark had risen right into the sun, leaving only its song to show where it had gone.

'All things bright and beautiful!' sang the old man, and Robbie skipped ahead of him, happy as a swallow.

Kincaple Farm was set halfway up a hill – a clutter of buildings, some red-roofed with endless waves of pantiles, and some, like the big cattleshed, clad with blue slates.

Across from this shed was the cattleman's house, its gable-end close to the road.

Below the upper window, were stuck sea-shells in the shape of a crown and painted red, white and blue. And on either side of the crown was written, again in cockleshells from the Eden estuary,

'ER 1953.'

It was the work of the cattleman and his wife, and it had taken the whole village by surprise that Coronation summer two years before.

But it wasn't the crown that drew Robbie and his grandfather that morning.

As they approached the farm, they saw the cattleman's wife standing in the roadway, sleeves rolled up her pink, ham-like arms, hands on hips, stamping angry.

And as they got nearer, they saw it. The bruise – a fierce blue welt that split her face!

'Have you sheen him?' she cried in a strangled sort of a voice, for speech seemed a sore and difficult thing for her. 'Have you sheen our Shandy?'

Robbie and the old man shook their heads.

'I'll shkin the young devil!' she shrieked on. 'Him and hish blashted gowf!'

The links of St Andrews were less than three miles away, and young Sandy had been fair taken with the Open there a month or two before. He'd been playing his own imaginary game against the champion Peter Thomson – with a walking stick on the washing green!

All young Sandy had needed to beat the great man was a good drive – but unknown to the lad, his mother had moved in close behind him as she pegged out her washing.

24

He was a big lad for his age, and his swing had been far too vigorous. Sandy had caught his toe in a tussock of grass and his mother, who had peeped out from behind a white, cotton sheet, had been struck full in the face with a smack like the crack of a whip!

The crook of the stick had left her with a bruise from ear to ear, and she wore it on her face like a daftie's smile!

But smiling she was not!

'I'll short the young devil! When I get my handsh on him I'll – I'll –'

The sentence was left unfinished as she whirled and fluttered off in her apron, clomping away in turned-down wellies to search the farm.

On the grass of the washing green a crooked stick and a spilled basket lay abandoned.

When Robbie looked up at his grandfather, the old man was biting on his lip and little tears were squeezing out from the corners of his eyes.

It was some time before he dared speak, lest the laughter broke free.

'Well, Robbie,' he tried at length, his voice trembling. 'Do you fanshy going to shee the engine?'

'Yesh,' said Robbie, and the pair of them gave in to helpless giggling.

The cattleman's wife never heard them, but most of the morning Robbie and his grandfather heard her – screeching through the buildings, banging doors and throwing heavy things aside.

The engine stood out in the open in a stone-walled yard at the foot of the farm. It was about the biggest thing Robbie had ever set eyes on, and the parts that weren't brass were dark, secret shades of greens and reds.

Although it was exposed to the rains and the winds and the snows, there was little rust to it, except for on the rims of the huge iron wheels, which hadn't moved for nearly ten years, since the old man had retired.

There had been no further need for either Robbie's grandfather or the machine. The threshing mill was no longer a thing that had to be hauled to the fields, for the harvest was now brought to the farm, to a new mill housed in a building all of its own. An ordinary tractor could drive the belt for it, and there was even talk of it getting a generator of its own to power it electrically.

Grass had taken a grip of the stilled wheels, and a couple of springtimes ago, a pair of cushie-doos had nested in the tall, stack chimney. The old man had cleaned it out and covered it over with wire netting once the squabs had grown and left.

It was a 1922 Fowler Steam Driven Traction Engine, but it was much more than that to Robbie's grandfather.

It had been a part of him, his pride and his joy and even now, when he had times of loneliness, it still had the power to cheer him up, to lift him as he remembered the days gone by when he'd been up there, behind the levers and the valves and the taps and the gauges, feeling the sharp blast of the heat on his legs from the furnace, and the cold draught of the great spinning flywheel that spun the belt for the threshing mill.

'Ah, Robbie,' he sighed. 'Man, it was something! When I had full power on and the belt was whistling through the still air on an autumn morning, it was like – like some great ocean-going liner with me the only one on board and the whole seven seas to myself!'

He delved into the tool-box at the back of the platform they were standing on and pulled out an oiled rag, which he used to wipe clear a pressure valve.

Although Robbie didn't fully realise why it all meant so much to his grandfather, he well understood that it did – and he knew the right questions to ask to get the old man smiling and talking, waving his arms in the air as he recalled bygone feats.

'What's the steam like?' asked Robbie, starting the game.

'Low,' was the old man's reply, as he tapped the cracked glass with his knuckles. 'It's more coal we need – and quick!'

Robbie heaped imaginary shovelsful of coal into the furnace.

'We'll need all the power we can get,' went on his grandfather. 'There's only another couple of stacks left in the yard – we can finish the threshing today and be done with it!'

Robbie piled on more fuel, then slammed the cast-iron door shut with his boot.

The old man pulled at stiff levers, his hands trembling with excitement.

'Aye,' he said, away again. 'It was something. I mind when I used to haul the shepherd's caravan up the hills at lambing time, up to the high fields near Strathkinness. And it took it no bother. Not fast, mind you – but not slow either. Just steady like. And it could have done it all day long and through the night as well if there had been the need . . .'

He was well away now. And Robbie, too. He could almost feel it hum and move beneath him as the old man tapped at dials and checked valves and eased levers off their ratchets.

'More steam!' he cried again. 'Come on, Robbie – you're dreaming there!'

At that very instant, in the middle of their secret game, young Geordie Lee bounced past the yard on his shining new David Brown tractor.

He braked to a halt in a swirl of stoor, then reversed and called up.

'Ahoy there, Captain! Bet you wish you had a real tractor like this one instead of that old heap!' he yelled. 'There's a fair few bob's worth of scrap there, all right!'

Then he crunched his tractor into gear and roared away again, laughing.

From that very second, the magic seemed to melt away like the bloom from a fresh-picked poppy.

The old man smiled a tired sort of smile and shrugged. He placed a hand on the boy's shoulder.

'Come on then, laddie,' he said softly. 'The tide must be on the turn now – we'll go down and see if there's any fish!'

At low water, the estuary of the River Eden seemed the bleakest, loneliest place in all the world.

It was wide and flat and had drained empty but for a narrow bit ribbon in the centre.

The mussel beds near Chisholm's Point had dried out grey in the sun, and the shells grated and crunched as Robbie and his grandfather walked over them to where the salmon boat would beach.

Suddenly, from the far side of the empty estuary, with a roar that seemed to rip the sky in two, a silver jet streaked above the forests of Tentsmuir.

'Look – a Hunter!' yelled Robbie through the din. 'Just look at him go!'

Hawker Hunters were still quite new to the skies around the air station at Leuchars. Over the years, the locals had grown used to the quieter jets – the whining Vampires which everybody called 'sackbarrows' because of their funny-looking twin tails, the Meteors and the Canberras – but the Hunters were different.

Real fighters, they were! Sleek like darts and fast! So fast that more than a few times they dived down and through the sound barrier, with a boom that rocked the whole countryside, sending cattle and sheep scattering for cover – and sending angry farmers leaping to their telephones to roar and bellow their disapproval!

Robbie and the old man watched as the plane thundered into the sky, leaving the runways far behind. Within seconds, it had shrunk to a tiny speck in the blue, catching the sun on its wings for an instant, before growling away into nothingness far, far out over the North Sea.

A flock of oyster-catchers, which had banked off in alarm at the sudden rush of noise, settled down again just as quickly and got busy once more scuttling along the edges of the lapping waters, poking and prodding for sandworms.

Beyond them, pulling steadily on creaking, slapping oars, were two men in a long coble boat. At the bows were high folds of green nets and coils of corked rope.

At the stern, covered with a square of jute sacking, was a box.

Robbie and his grandfather leaned forward and held the prow steady as the keel scrunched onto the shingle and the two men stepped out into the shallows.

'A good day, was it, boys?' asked the old man, panting with the effort of holding the boat against the currents.

'No' bad,' nodded the elder of the salmon netters. 'But no' what it's been, either. I can mind a Lammastime not long after the war there when the salmon and finnock were moving up shoulder to shoulder, and we thought the boat was going to tip with the weight of them all in the nets.'

The younger man, a sturdy, beetroot-faced lad with a tumble of fair curls, lifted some oilskins from the boat and laid them across his arm. With his free hand, he pointed out towards the mouth of the river.

'Thon's what's wrong, these days,' he grumbled. 'Too many o' them things.'

In the distance, lying like full sacks of grain on the sandbanks, were seals. There must have been fifty at least, and the heads of many more bobbed up and down in the waters beside them.

'It's a wonder there's any fish left for us at all by the time they've had their fill,' went on the young lad.

But fish there were – and Robbie and his grandfather helped the salmon netters haul their box like a sledge across the mudflats, up the shore, to where the van was parked.

When the damp sacking was lifted off the box, Robbie's breath fair whistled from him! There were a dozen or more fish in the box, and even all the treasures of King Solomon would have lost their sparkle beside them!

The older man bent down, hooked two fingers into the maroon gills of one of the salmon and hoisted it up and out of the box.

He laughed like a pirate as he laid it across Robbie's arms.

'Well, laddie – and what do you think of this one, eh?'

It was easily the best fish of the whole catch, and must have weighed twenty pounds and more. Robbie could feel his arms strain and tremble with the effort of holding it – a gleaming block of solid silver, studded with jewels of green and blue and red and purple. And when he let it slap back down into the box with the others, he saw that the sleeves of his jerkin were covered with scales, like a thousand glistening, shimmering sequins.

Robbie never even tried to brush them off, but kept looking at them, letting the sunlight dance across them, fair taken with their beauty.

The dust raised by the netter's van settled slowly back onto the track as Robbie and the old man made to follow for home.

They took their time, for their time was their own to take, and there was so much to do with it.

Like looking at the sandmartins, who had scraped out their nesting holes high in the soft bankings at the edge of the estuary. The young from the early broods had learned to fly and were already masters of the air – wheeling, darting, dipping and skimming, and all the while chittering with the sheer pleasure it gave them.

Soon, in a month or so, they would gather together in countless thousands to fly South, taking the last of the warm days with them.

Then, a hare got up from the side of the track, springing from its form in the long grass and away.

Robbie gave chase and his grandfather's laughter crackled in the air. The boy had no chance, and knew it, but he ran all the same, jumping, skipping, waving his arms, and tumbling in the soft, warm grass, and all to please the old man.

Ahead of him, the hare twisted and turned, leaping in great bounds and away.

When Robbie at last came back, the old man, still chuckling, was crouched on one knee, folding the grass back, gently, carefully.

'That's where he was – I bet it's still warm.'

Robbie put his hand in the hollow, feeling the mossy floor

lightly with his knuckles. It was warm. And then, amazingly, he felt something else, something strange and it was a shining sixpence.

And when he asked his grandfather, the old man shook his head and said he knew nothing about it and that it just went to show what funny creatures hares could be!

And Robbie didn't know what to think!

The old man was still smiling and the young boy still puzzling – when they sensed it together!

It wasn't the noise that startled them, for the noise was yet to come.

It was more a feeling, a sudden awareness of something moving at terrific speed.

Theirs was the feeling of a mouse when the talons of the kestrel are but inches from him – or a rabbit with the hot breath of a fox on its neck!

A heart-stopping, lurch of a feeling!

The Hunter was back!

The jet raced its flickering shadow across the estuary, slicing silently through the air, then banking off towards Balmullo Hill.

In an instant, the sound followed like a wall of water bursting from a dam, a roar that set the oyster-catchers wheeling again, and made Robbie and the old man clamp their hands to their ears as the ground shuddered beneath them.

Up and up and up the plane soared, looping over high above. Then down and over the runways of Leuchars again, this time twisting and turning like a hungry swallow through the clouds of midges that hung and danced above the trees on summer evenings.

Again the roar went hammering after the plane, flooding the whole estuary with sound.

And again the plane screamed overheard, but this time, as it sat back on its tail to soar, there came a loud crack and a veil of light grey smoke was left hanging in the air behind it!

Robbie and the old man watched, horrified, as the plane

31

– instantly silent – lurched nose up, sliding gracelessly across the sky.

There was another crack, and a small, black object spun up and away from the jet.

'The pilot!' yelled Robbie. 'He's ejected! The plane's coming down!'

Instinctively, the boy and the old man flung themselves to the ground.

The jet tilted and tumbled in cartwheels. Down and down it came, no longer the thing of beauty, but clumsy, ungainly, doomed.

With a great slap, it bellyflopped onto the mud of the estuary. The impact shot it up into the air again in a huge spray of muck and water and for a split second, it seemed to stay there, like a great leaping fish.

Robbie looked up and saw the red, white and blue roundels on the undersides of its wings as it hung in the air, then, spent, it flopped back down onto the mud, slithering to a halt, far out.

The pilot swung quickly to the ground, slanting into the rough grass less than a hundred yards from Robbie and his grandfather. Already, alarm bells were sounding across the estuary from the airfield, and by the time the boy and the old man reached the pilot, a siren was wailing.

He'd been lucky. If it hadn't been for his ejector seat, the pilot wouldn't have had a chance, for he'd been too close to the ground to have given him time to open his cockpit, leap clear and pull the cord of his parachute.

But when the engine had cut out, he'd been able to pull down the handle above his head and had set off the explosive charges which had fired his entire seat unit up and away from the stricken aircraft.

A tiny parachute had blossomed and had tugged out the main one, and so he'd been saved.

But it had been close – very close, and the landing had been hard and awkward.

When Robbie and his grandfather reached him, the pilot was lying half on his side, with his right leg twisted beneath him.

They helped him unclasp the catch on his harness, then laid him gently down.

'My leg . . . it's broken,' the pilot gasped shakily. Then he grinned, and ran a hand back through his moist hair as he looked out to where the Hawker Hunter lay.

'Still . . . it could have been worse . . . a lot worse . . .'

At that, he leaned back into the grass and lay silently looking up into the depths of the blue sky.

The old man, close to exhaustion after the race across the rough ground and trembling as the shock of it all began to grip and squeeze tight, sank down beside him.

Robbie gathered in the silky folds of the parachute, then he too sat down to wait.

The airfield at Leuchars was less than a mile away across the estuary of the Eden, but the convoy of grey vehicles had to speed the long way round, clanging and wailing and flashing through Guardbridge, then swinging left onto the main St Andrews road before turning off down the rough track that went to the shore.

An ambulance led the way, bucking and bumping across the uneven ground, twisting through clumps of whin that showered golden petals to the ground as it brushed by.

Then a fire engine, then a big truck with a dozen or so men in it, and finally, a jeep containing a driver and two officers — very important looking men with peaked caps and with rings on their sleeves that reminded Robbie of stripy liquorice allsorts.

One of the officers rushed around, yelling out orders, pointing, waving his arms, and calling everyone 'Chappie'.

The other said not a word.

The pilot was placed carefully onto a stretcher and was put into the ambulance.

Then, just before the double doors were closed, he raised himself up on one elbow, saluted, and said 'Thank you'.

Robbie felt ten feet tall as he saluted back, then, with a final wave, the pilot was gone.

Two of the men from the truck, carrying a perspex cockpit canopy between them, set out across the mud.

'We must keep out as much water and silt as we can,' the

33

officer called after them. 'The salvage chappies will be down from Lossiemouth tomorrow morning, but the old kite will be under water tonight.'

Some more men trudged and squelched out with covers for the jet's intakes and outlet. They had to hurry, for already the tide was pushing in.

After that, there was nothing more to do, nothing more to see until all the fun of the next day, so once again, Robbie and his grandfather set off for home.

News of the crash had spread like a blaze in a stackyard, and all the way back up the road, groups of sightseers hurried by, pointing, chattering, anxious to see the plane, hoping to see the pilot, eager to see anything.

Tagging along at the back of one of the groups was Sandy, the cattleman's son. In spite of all the clamour and excitement around him, he seemed to be in no great hurry, but walked rather slowly, stiffly – perhaps even sorely . . .

Robbie and his grandfather nodded as Sandy hirpled by.

'Oh, Sandy,' said the old man all innocent like. 'We met your mother earlier – she seemed quite anxious to have a word with you about something or other. Did she get you all right?'

The look on Sandy's face told the whole story. His mother had got him all right – hiding among the sacks in the granary.

He'd been white with meal dust when she'd hauled him out, but by the time she'd finished with him, every last speck had been beaten off.

It would be a while before Sandy challenged for the Open Championship again – but he still managed a smile for Robbie and the old man.

The night was slow in passing, like a Christmas Eve, with all the excitement and expectation of the day to come.

Robbie and his grandfather spun out their tasks to help the time go by, spending each one slowly and wisely.

The pig was given its evening meal, and the hens were boarded in, safely shut away from the rats and foxes.

Then the boy and the old man turned to the woodpile, and began to saw up a few logs.

Winter was a long way away, but firewood had to be gathered in well before it arrived, for it was no job to leave for the cold, damp days. A little every now and then, and the pile in the woodshed soon swelled.

Robbie stood on a box at the far side of the saw-cuddy as he and the old man pulled the long saw blade back and forwards between them, rasping through a limb of ashwood.

'It's grand stuff, this,' smiled the old man as the note of the saw sank lower. He was already dreaming of blazing fires when the logs were piled on end in the grate and the flames were roaring and cold winter was left to howl and shiver on the doorstep.

'Burns just like coal does ash, and after it's gone, you just tap it with the poker and it disappears – no mess, nothing.'

Then when the branch was done and the logs were chopped into quarters and stacked to air, Robbie followed his grandfather to the cottage.

It was virtually a single room, with his high bed in the far corner and a chair at the fireside – all he needed.

He ate his meals round at Robbie's, but still chose to sleep under his own roof.

The old man eased out a long sigh as he leaned his back into the cushions. Then, when the silence had grown long between them, and he found himself going over the day again, he gave his grandson a nudge.

'Come on,' he winked. 'You can give me a wee tune.'

Robbie took the mouth organ from the tin on the mantelpiece, tapped it a couple of times in the palm of his hand, then sat down by the fender.

He played all the tunes he knew, and his grandfather's favourites twice and more.

At 'Rowan Tree', the old man sang to a faded wedding photo that hung on the wall near the fire. Any words he forgot were made up or hummed over.

And when Robbie stirred into 'Cock O' The North', the old man's foot began to tap in time, and the boy felt glad to see it.

And when 'Bonnie Dundee' followed, Robbie's grandfather got up, crossed to the press, and from a drawer, selected a pair of spoons

He held them in his hand, back to back, and ran them over his fingers and on his knee and up and down his arm, ringing and rattling out rhythms like hail dirling on a tin roof.

And so the night reeled and whirled away. And when Robbie finally went home to bed, he was tired and gave in quickly to sleep, stirring for only a second as he thought, dreaming already, what funny creatures hares could be . . .

For some strange reason, Robbie had half-expected the plane to be gone by morning. It had all seemed so unreal that he wasn't sure if it had happened at all, and that it had all been a dream, somehow.

But it was no dream, and the plane was still there, on the mud, far out.

The salvage crew from Lossiemouth had arrived in two big trucks, and a long steel cable had been fed out from the winch on one of the lorries to the jet.

The same two officers were in charge, the one still silent, and the other still bobbing around like a watery-wagtail.

Sergeant Baxter, the Local Police Force himself, had pedalled his bike along the road from his office in Guardbridge, and he nodded as Robbie and the old man passed.

'So it's still here, then?' remarked Robbie's grandfather to him. 'I thought somebody might have pinched it in the night!'

Sergeant Baxter snorted.

'They had a guard on it!' he declared solemnly, before it occurred to him the old man was teasing.

'Chappie' by this time was waving a white handkerchief in the air, signalling to the men out at the jet.

Robbie and the old man watched.

In the distance, out on the mud, the men waved back.

'They're ready!' announced the officer. 'Right, chappie,' he called to the winchman on the salvage lorry. 'You can start taking in the slack whenever I raise my arm.'

The arm, with the liquorice allsort rings on the sleeve, was raised slowly into the air.

In an instant, the lorry's motor revved, and the drum began to turn, winding in the slack.

'Keep clear a'body!' yelled Sergeant Baxter, the Local Police Force, to the clumps of spectators who were scattered along the shoreline.

The lorry revved louder, and the cable tightened more. It shimmered and quivered like a bowstring, dripping droplets of silver water all along its length.

The drum began to creak and groan.

All eyes were fixed on the Hunter out in the mud.

Then . . . slowly . . . slowly . . . it began to move! No, not the jet – but the salvage lorry! It slipped and slithered, then sunk up to its axles in the soft, boggy ground!

From one of the groups of onlookers, there came a jackdaw-like cackle of laughter, but there was no such sign of amusement on the faces of the salvage crew.

Or the officers!

A photographer from the Dundee Courier clicked his camera and caught them glowering like they'd just been slapped with a wet haddock!

'Chappie' went red, then purple, then stalked over to the stricken lorry.

The salvage crew and the rest of the airmen gathered round scratching their heads, frowning, muttering strange mutterings.

The driver swung up into his cab and crunched the lorry into gear. The wheels spun freely round, spewing out mud behind them, and the lorry sank further, settling like a broody hen on her eggs!

Shovelfuls of grit and gravel were fetched from the shore and slung under the tyres, but it made no difference, there was no grip.

'Right, chappies!' came the cry. 'All hands to the back!'

And Robbie and the old man, like everyone else, joined in, heaving and shoving as the engine note rose high in the morning air.

But still nothing happened.

Then suddenly, the old man straightened up, his face strained and drawn.

'Grandfather!' cried Robbie. 'What's wrong?'

The old man said nothing, just stood bent with his hands on his knees.

'You should take it easy at your age,' advised Sergeant Baxter, himself red in the face and panting.

Robbie's grandfather waited till the breath came back to his body.

'I – I'm fine,' he managed. 'Don't you worry now, Robbie – but I think I'll take a wee wander up the road for a bit . . .'

'I'll come with you,' the boy said.

The old man smiled a tired smile, his face still ashen.

'No – no, there's no need. I'll be all right. You wait here and give them a hand. I'll be back down.'

And with no more than that, he was away.

Robbie watched him go, and the worry grew in the boy like winter darkness. He'd never really thought of his grandfather as being old – he was just always there somehow. Always had been, and always would be.

But he was old and frail, and sometimes he seemed so tired and far away . . .

Robbie was about to run and catch him up when he saw that the old man had reached the main road, and at that very moment, a tractor and trailer had pulled up to offer him a lift up the hill.

Before he clambered up onto the back, the old man turned and waved his stick cheerily in the air and Robbie felt a bit better. He turned back to watch the fun.

Some lengths of steel matting were produced from the back of the second truck, and they were wedged under the spinning tyres. But to no avail – the ground was too soft and there was still no grip.

Then 'Chappie' called for channels to be dug out in front of the wheels to give them a bit of a run, but that didn't work either.

Then another cable was hitched to the back of the second

lorry. It too revved and roared and squirmed from side to side as it strained against its load, but nothing moved.

And all the while, 'Chappie' fluttered about, ordering this, ordering that, moving men to the front, to the back, and to the sides – but all in vain.

And so it went on for an hour or more, and all the time the tide was turning, creeping nearer and nearer and nearer.

Then suddenly, above all the yelling and revving and grinding – a new noise was heard.

Chuff-chuff-chuff-chuff-chuff-chuff-chuff!

And coming down the track, smoke belching into the blue skies, was a 1922 Fowler Steam Driven Traction Engine! Robbie raced up the rough road to meet it.

'Grandfather! Grandfather!' he called, his heart pounding like the mighty engine itself.

The old man held out a hand and heaved the boy up onto the platform beside him.

'Grandfather!' cried Robbie again. 'Why did you not tell me? I could have come too! I could have helped you!'

The old man pushed a lever and eased back the steam a shade.

'Oh, Robbie!' he shouted, with tears of happiness shining in his eyes. 'I did want you with me, laddie – but, but if it hadn't started and you were there I – I couldn't have faced it!'

Robbie clung in close to the old man, and he felt the arms tighten around him.

'But it started all right – after all that time, it started all right!' laughed the grandfather. 'Now come on – we've a job of work to do! More coal! More coal!'

Robbie grabbed the shovel and piled some coal into the furnace. The heat belted out at him, snatching the breath from him.

Then the old man pulled a lever and they were away.

Great gasps of steam sighed from the boiler, pushing, pushing, pushing the pistons and driving the wheels, slowly, slowly but so surely.

The traction engine trundled on, creeping like some pre-historic monster across the rough ground.

A dog barked at it and came snarling close, but then thought better of it and ran off with its tail tucked in between its legs.

'Unhook the cable!' the old man called down to the officers. 'I'll haul your lorry out first!'

'Are you sure you can do it, chappie?'

Robbie's grandfather grinned.

'Unhook your cable,' was all he said.

Some men disconnected the winch, then hooked a chain from the back of the traction engine to the front of the salvage lorry.

'Stand back!' cried the old man as he took up the strain.

The engine chuffed louder and louder, pulling, pulling, pulling.

The links on the chain drew trembling tight.

Then with a great slurp, the salvage lorry was hauled free from the clinging grip of the mud.

The local press photographer danced round and round and round, snapping from every angle.

'Now your cable!' yelled Robbie's grandfather. 'Fix it to the winch underneath here and I'll get your wee aeroplane out while I'm at it!'

Again the salvage men milled around like worker bees in a hive, carrying out the instructions just as fast as they were able.

'We'll need all the power we can get now!' the old man called to Robbie.

He pulled open a valve, and tapped his knuckles hard against a pressure gauge. The steam hissed and roared around them, and the great flywheel hummed like a hive.

Beneath it, the gearwheels grated and turned into each other, biting, biting, biting.

The winch wheel underneath the traction engine's boiler groaned then turned, round and round and round, slowly, steadily reeling in the slack.

And then it was tight.

'Can he do it?' shouted Sergeant Baxter. The officers shrugged.

The 1922 Fowler Steam Driven Traction Engine shuddered under the strain.

For long moments, nothing seemed to be happening. Then suddenly . . . yes . . . yes . . . it was moving . . . the plane was moving!

Far out, the nose slewed round in the mud! Then, ever so slowly, the plane began to come in!

People rushed and pointed and jumped and cheered, and the dog barked and yelped and pranced on its hind legs!

On and on and on the plane came, and round and round and round went the winch, chewing the cable and swallowing it.

The smoke belched, the steam hissed and the old man watched. His hands – young again – flew to the controls, adjusting, easing, opening, coaxing.

And Robbie was with him. All the way. Beside him. Helping him.

Nearer and nearer came the Hunter, leaving a long trail across the mud of the estuary like a snail on a slab.

And then, amazingly, it was free of the mud and the muck and up onto the shingle, and then onto the grass beside them, huge and glistening.

The salvage crew and the officers and the airmen and all the spectators and Sergeant Baxter himself burst into applause.

Robbie looked up at the old man and saw the tears glinting in his eyes.

'Oh, Grandfather!' he cried, throwing his arms about him. 'I do love you so!'

And the old man held him tight.

And then it was home.

All the way up the road, the people cheered. The news raced on ahead of them, and everyone from the village ran out to see if it was true.

Folks lined the road and skipped alongside and somebody tied a bunch of streamers onto the engine like the ones that trailed from coaches on seaside outings.

And all the way home, all the way up the road, Robbie pulled on the string that blew the whistle.

And it blew. And it blew. And it blew . . .

THE HARVEST HOME

THE HARVEST was home.

The tree-lined roads around Kincaple no longer sounded to the steady rhythm of Clydesdales' hooves, the jingle-jangle of harness, and the creaking of carts laden high with fat sheaves.

Branches that hung low over the road were trailing wisps of straw, and pigeons, starlings and crows squabbled to feed on the grains that had sprinkled to the ground all the way to the farm.

For long autumn days, the men had laboured, pitching sheaves from the carts up to the builders who crawled round and round on their knees as the stacks grew higher and higher and higher.

Then, the tapering tops had been thatched with straw against the winds and the rains, and the whole thing had been roped and tied. On the last stack to be built, a straw cross was woven at the top, a symbol that the crop was in. The harvest was home.

'It's a fine like sight,' said Robbie's grandfather as he leaned against the wooden gate at the top end of the stackyard.

'And just think of the mice we can chase at threshing time!' said Robbie.

The old man laughed.

'And the rats! You'd better mind some string to tie around your trouser-legs! But here, we'd better hurry if we're to get ourselves all spruced up for the night! You're not forgetting, are you . . . ?'

Robbie snorted. Forget? Who could forget the night the whole farm held its breath for? The night when all the village danced and reeled and sang and birled! The night of the Harvest Home!

Robbie swung down from the gate and skipped after the old man . . .

A moon like a fat cheese had risen into the night sky when Robbie and his mother and his grandfather made their way down the hill to the farm.

It was a fine night, the whole countryside was still and quiet, and as they drew nearer to the silver shapes of the farm buildings, their steps grew lighter with excitement.

And then they heard it, all the way down the road, so faint at first they had to stop and turn their heads to the side, holding breath, listening hard . . . then louder and louder . . .

The music! Two accordions and a fiddle, that's all it was, but it quickened the heartbeat and sent a thrill dancing through the three of them as they walked.

A wedge of light shone from the crack-open door of the granary, and when Robbie's mother pulled it wide, the sound and brightness and magic of it all rushed out to welcome them and pulled them in!

It was like a palace!

The whole granary had been swept and scrubbed, and decorated with ribbons and streamers. Plank seating had been arranged, with a long table set up, running the whole length of the building. Ten tablecloths it took to cover it, so long it was!

And on it was piled heaps and heaps of food — hams and cheeses and roast ducks and geese and chickens, and bowls of salad and boiled potatoes, and brown-crusted bread, and scones and cakes all fresh and warm from the farmhouse kitchens!

It was like a right royal banquet.

And all around, all the folk from the village, dressed in their Sunday best, danced and swirled and chattered and laughed.

Robbie and his mother and his grandfather were swallowed up into the throng!

At the far end of the granary, hidden behind a jostling cluster of men, were bottles of whisky and rum, and bowls of punch and stone jars of beer, with lemonade and ginger beer for the children.

Keeping well clear of this corner was the great rolling figure of Will Fenton who, a couple of harvest homes before, had gone through an experience so terrible that it had driven him from the bottle for life!

He'd been supping all the night, and had slid further and further down the wall until, near midnight, he lay flat out on the wooden floorboards, with a bottle clasped to his chest and a smile fixed to his face.

Will was as bald as a swede neep, with a purple complexion to match, and as he lay on the floor, a plan was hatched . . .

Some of the men scampered round to the stables, giggling like schoolbairns. With a pair of shears, they'd cropped some hair from the tail of one of the horses.

Then, a few of the womenfolk had mixed up a flour and water paste and smeared it all over Will's bald pate. The hair was stuck on and slicked down just right, and then – not content with their devilment – they fashioned a beard and whiskers, too!

When Will stirred an hour or so later, there was a huddle of straight-faced folk around him who swore he'd been out cold for a week. The poor man was fair confused, and when a mirror was produced, he took one look at all the growth and passed right out again!

During his second coma, warm soapy water took all the hair away, and when Will recovered, no one even mentioned a thing about it. Will spent long minutes in front of his mirror, and even days and weeks later, he'd stop whatever it was he was doing in the field and rub his head and stroke his chin at the mystery of it all!

'Are you not having a wee nip?' asked Robbie's grandfather, all innocent like. 'It'll put hairs on your chest . . .'

A flicker of suspicion fluttered about Will Fenton's eyes as he shook his head. There was nothing that would coax him from his seat on the straw bale. The memory of it all made him shudder, and he was happy when the band struck up again, and his mind had something else to dwell on.

Jock Anderson was on the piano accordion, the very one he'd got from the great Jimmy Shand himself! Next to him, on the button-keyed box, was Pete Chalmers, with young Geordie Lee beside them, scraping on his fiddle.

All three were workers on the farm, and their hands were big and coarse and chapped, but their fingers fair danced across the notes and strings, and the granary was filled with the ringing of reels and jigs and polkas.

Behind the platform where the men played, hanging on the bare stone wall, was a single sheaf, the very last sheaf of the harvest. It was all done up, plaited and twined through with red, white and blue ribbons, and it was a sign that the year was over now that the harvest was in.

The sheaf would hang in the granary till the turn of the year, till the first day of the ploughing. Then, Rob Watson, the grieve, would take it down and the oats from it would be shared out as a tit-bit for the horses. And another year would start.

It was as he gazed up in admiration at the deft plaiting, that Robbie saw it. The movement, in the rafters. Somebody was moving about up there!

Robbie crept out of the granary door, away from the noise and the clamour, to the barn next door.

There, he scrambled up a mound of straw bales, crawled through a hole in the wall and there, on the granary rafters was – Sandy, the cattleman's son!

There was no way they could speak to each other, for the ring of an eightsome reel was swirling and rattling around the rafters beside them, but when Sandy saw Robbie, he beckoned him across and pointed down below, with a wicked grin tugging at the corners of his mouth!

The reel was at its wildest now, and in the middle of all the birling, was big Aggie Cunningham. Round and round she flew, with her man Tam, a wiry wee ploughman, hanging on to her elbow for dear life, his feet scarcely touching the floor as he whirled.

Aggie's dress swirled about her, and her muckle bosom heaved and walloped around. From above, it was like a pair

46

of piglets fighting, and the two boys nudged and poked each other, giggling and tee-heeing at each mighty heave!

And then the reel was ended, and breathless, the dancers staggered back for rest and refreshment.

With an almost theatrical sense of timing, the door burst open and in came the Reverend Arbuckle from the Parish of Strathkinness. He was a tall man, and skinny as a twig, with a tight face and a stern look. He was for all the world like a heron.

The granary fell hushed at the sight of the figure with the long black coat-tails flapping around the thin, black-gaitered legs. So quiet was it that, even from their perch up in the rafters, Robbie and Sandy could hear the squeak of his black, leather shoes.

The Reverend Arbuckle stalked over to the platform where the band stood, shook hands with a few of the folk there, then spread his arms out wide below the decorated sheaf.

'Let us pray!' he sang in a high, nasal tone. And all heads were bowed.

It was at this precise second that Sandy, high above it all, saw the dead mouse. It lay just a couple of feet away on a rafter.

A look of mischief twinkled in his eyes like the first star of a frosty night!

He leaned forward and picked up the stiff, little corpse by the tail. Below, the muckle bosom of big Aggie Cunningham was still heaving after the reel . . .

Sandy bit at his lip to keep the excitement from bursting out. He winked at Robbie.

'Watch this . . .' he whispered.

'Oh Lord, we thank Thee for another year . . .'

Sandy edged forward along the rafters . . .

'And for the seed that grew strong . . .'

Robbie watched, scarcely daring to draw breath, as the cattleman's son crept on . . .

'Let us be like the seed. Let us pray that we, too, will grow straight and strong . . .'

Sandy was well out now. He looked down at the bowed

heads below. He was directly above the swede neep of Will Fenton – a fine target, right enough – but there was something better to aim at . . .

'And that we ripen in the warm sun of righteousness . . .'

Big Aggie Cunningham quietly took out a cologne-soaked handkerchief from her handbag and dabbed at herself. Almost directly above her, a stealthy figure crept nearer and nearer . . .

'Yeah, Lord, we thank Thee for so much this year. But most of all, we thank Thee for . . .'

Sandy stretched out . . . just one more rafter to cross . . .

'For Thy bounteous gifts from above!'

There was a crack, a scream, a howl – and a boy clutching a dead mouse by the tail plunged from the rafters and fell head first into a bowl of salad!

THE PIG

THE PIG was fat.

Its diet of scraps and meal and boiled potatoes had given it bulk enough, and with it being October time, a month with an 'r' in it when the heat of the summer had faded, plans could be made for the creature's demise.

Robbie's grandfather was well in with Murray the butcher in the market town of Cupar, which lay about eight miles to the west of Kincaple, and for a bottle of Bell's whisky, the man had agreed to slaughter the beast, and to bleed it, scauld it and scrape it, and to cut it and cure it and smoke it as well.

All Robbie's grandfather had to do was to deliver it.

And that was where Tasker came in.

Tasker was a pinched-faced little man, with big, sticky-out ears like a Baby Austin with its doors open. His hair was as black as a bucket of melted tar, and was kept in place with a slick of Brylcreem, which somehow managed to give his whole face a shiny look.

Slippery would be the word for Tasker if he was of a criminal nature, but he was not – his many deals and transactions were on the right side of the law, but sometimes only just. Whenever someone in the village got a bargain of cheap coal, or new working boots for less than half price, or car tyres, or anything that had 'fallen off the back of a lorry', it was usually Tasker's lorry they were referring to.

His jobs were many and various. From his tar-painted sheds near Guardbridge, he conducted a whole range of businesses – blacksmith, mechanic, scrap metal dealer, tyre fitter, saw setter, chimney sweep and – seeing as he had an Albion lorry, he went in for a bit of removal work as well.

Even pig removing – and for a bottle of Bell's whisky, he'd agreed to transport the old man's pig on its last journey.

Robbie tipped a pailful of mash into the trough and he and his grandfather watched from the wall of the sty as the pig slurped through its last supper.

'I'll be a bit sorry to see him go tomorrow, Grandfather,' said the boy. 'He's been a right canny sort – not like that wild thing we had the last time!'

'Aye . . . I'll be a bit sorry myself,' mused the old man, and he took a long draw from his pipe. Then a faint smile came to his lips.

'But, here, we'd better watch what we're doing, for you know what happens if you shed tears over a pig . . .'

Robbie frowned. 'What happens?'

'It makes the bacon fair salty!'

The pair of them laughed and then left the pig in peace.

The old man was washed and shaved and ready by the time Robbie got round to his place next morning. Tasker had yet to appear, so the pair of them sat by the fire, sipping at hot, sweet tea from mugs, waiting for the knock.

It came.

'Where's your lorry? We never heard it coming,' said the old man at the doorstep.

An unlit stub of a cigarette hung at the side of Tasker's mouth. It was to stay there throughout all the excitement that the day was to bring.

'I've left it round the corner,' said Tasker, the Woodbine bobbing. 'Except it's not my lorry.'

The old man looked puzzled.

'Rear axle's gone on the Albion,' went on Tasker. 'Still, I've got something else. I'm doing a servicing job for the Co-operative.'

'Oh, the Co-operative lorry – that's fair posh,' exclaimed the old man, tickled with the idea of travelling in their new Austin.

The early morning sun flashed on Tasker's shining head as

he shook it, deepening the mystery. 'No – no, it's not the lorry. It's – it's . . .'

Robbie and his grandfather gaped round the corner. Drawn up at the end of the row of cottages, sombre black paintwork and sparkling chrome, was – the Co-operative hearse!

'In the name! We can't use that thing!' gasped the old man.

'Sure we can,' said Tasker.

'But – but it's a hearse!'

'It'll be all right,' insisted Tasker. 'I've got some straw in the back. They're no' needing it today, anyway!'

'They'll be needing it for me if there's much more of this!' exclaimed Robbie's grandfather.

But Tasker was unruffled by it all.

'I could say I was road-testing it if anybody saw us,' he said, matter-of-fact like.

'But – with a pig?' insisted the old man.

'Och, I could say that was to simulate working conditions . . .'

'Ah, well . . . if you're sure then,' shrugged the old man. 'But I'm no' very happy about it. I can see us getting the jail if we're caught . . .'

But Tasker's assurances that things would be all right won the old man over, and soon, they were hunting around for some planks and some boarding to make a ramp.

Then Tasker backed the hearse up to the door of the sty, and with the help of a bowl of mash and a couple of sticks, the pig was coaxed, bullied and persuaded up and into the back.

And then they were off, with Robbie, his grandfather and Tasker in the front, and a hundredweight and more of live pork in the back!

The journey had begun!

Slowly, so as not to upset the temperamental cargo, the hearse made its way through the village of Kincaple, down the hill past the farm, then turned left onto the main Guardbridge to Cupar road.

'See?' grinned Tasker, tempting Providence, 'I told you

it would be easy! There's not a thing to worry about!'

But there was!

For who should see them approach the road junction at Guardbridge but Sergeant Baxter, the local police force himself!

He was off his bicycle in a flash and out into the middle of the road with his hand held high.

'I knew it!' declared Robbie's grandfather. 'We're caught – we've had it – it'll be the jail for us all!'

But it wasn't the hearse that Sergeant Baxter was flagging down. Instead, he held his arm aloft to stop the flow of cars coming from the Newport road, from the ferry across the Tay. And with his free hand, he beckoned the hearse on!

With a ceremonious deliberation, Sergeant Baxter removed the cap from his head.

Tasker waited until he was almost level, then thumped his foot hard down. The hearse sailed by, leaving the poor policeman wide-eyed and gaping, and the traffic peeping and tooting at his birling, bewildered form in the middle of the road!

The hearse still rang with Tasker's crazy laughter when it nosed into Cupar.

Murray's shop was in the main market street, the Crossgate, and the black, sombre vehicle swung silently up the cobbled close that led to the backyard.

'Made it!' announced Tasker, killing the engine. 'Did I not tell you we would?'

Robbie's grandfather leaned his back into the plush leather seat, took off his cap and ran the back of his hand across his brow.

The fat form of Murray the butcher filled the entrance to his backyard, and his chins wobbled like a turkey's wattle as his jaw fell open at the sight of the hearse.

'Come on,' said the old man, not wishing to waste time with explanations. 'Let's get the thing out and be done with it. I'm just not happy about this at all . . .'

His feelings of unease, as things turned out, were totally justified, for it was outside the rear entrance to Murray's shop that disaster struck!

Just as Tasker had prepared some ramps and had lifted up the back door of the hearse, the pig got a sniff of something in the air that it definitely did not take to!

With a great squeal, it lunged down the ramp like a liner on a slipway, clattering and slithering on the cobbles, knocking Tasker, Robbie, the old man and even Murray to one side in its mad dash for liberty!

They looked up just in time to see the creature's vast, pink backside disappearing out of the yard door and away!

In an instant, the three men and the boy were on their feet and in pursuit.

Being a Saturday, the Crossgate was already filling up with shoppers, and they scattered in all directions as the runaway pig came thundering along the pavements, its great lugs flapping about its eyes, blinding it in its frantic bid for freedom.

Behind, Robbie, the old man, Murray and Tasker came pelting in the chase.

There were a few stalls at the top end of the street – vegetables, and flowers, and basketware, things like that – and it was with a terrible feeling of impending disaster that they saw the pig charging towards them.

'Oh no!' gasped Robbie's grandfather, clutching onto a lamp-post for support.

For a sweet second, the pig seemed to veer away, but then its flapping ears blocked its vision again and it changed course, bang on target for the middle of the stalls.

There came a great clatter, and a cascade of crimson and yellow chrysanthemums showered into the air like a glorious firework. And then pots and pans and various vegetables and squawking chickens!

And all accompanied by a rising roar from the swarm of shoppers and stall-holders that scattered about in complete confusion.

And still the chase went on! But the beast was running out of road now, and was near to the top end of the street.

It turned, lifted its snout, and from below the fringes of its lugs, it could just make out the closing figures of the boy

53

and the men. With a desperate final lunge it dived for cover into the nearest opening it could find.

Its vast pinkness disappeared right into Miss Purdom's drapery store!

'Have you seen a pig?' asked Tasker inside.

Miss Purdom, bespectacled, and gawky as a pullet, said nothing, but the fact that she was standing on the shop-counter with a stricken look to her face was answer enough. She jabbed a bony finger at the curtain covering the entrance to the back shop.

Tasker, Robbie, the old man and Murray crept forward. Cautiously, Tasker unhooked the curtain.

In the middle of the floor, with a peach-coloured piece of satin frivolity draped around it, stood the pig.

Its pink eye was on them, and then beyond them, looking for an exit. But Tasker was too quick. He grabbed the curtain and leapt forward, covering the pig's head. It bucked and thrashed about, squealing and stamping and struggling, but all in vain.

They roped it, and the poor beast was dragged out of the shop, past the muttering stall-holders trying to salvage what wares they could, along the Crossgate, and back into the butcher's yard.

Its time of freedom was over.

But the pig had one last gesture to make. One last kick against humanity – except that it wasn't a kick. It was a bite. And poor Tasker, bending down to tighten a lace that had worked loose in the chase, was at the sharp end of it!

He clutched at his backside and howled high into the air.

If ever a pig went on its last journey with a feeling of achievement and contentment inside it, it was that one.

As for Tasker, he sat and shifted awkwardly on an inflated inner-tube for long weeks after.

In fact, he was still getting the occasional twinge a couple of months later, after the old man had taken delivery of the cured and smoked pork and hams from Murray. Robbie and his grandfather walked down from Kincaple to the tar-painted sheds near Guardbridge.

The old man placed a large, brown paper parcel on Tasker's bench.

'It's a bit pork,' he said. 'From the hind quarters. I thought you might like to do unto the pig as he did unto you!'

THE SCHOOL BUS

THE ROAD THAT LED DOWN from the village of Kincaple was rough and winding. It twisted like a kite-tail, and over many years, had been worn and rutted by great iron-rimmed cartwheels, and by the heavy hooves of Clydesdale work horses.

It was down this rough road that Robbie hurtled every school morning.

Robbie's arrival!

At twenty-five minutes to nine, Mondays to Fridays, the school bus chugged along towards the Kincaple road-end – the last but one stop on its stuttering journey to school in St Andrews.

And at twenty-five minutes to nine, Mondays to Fridays, Robbie vaulted into the saddle of his bicycle and set off to meet it!

At the first sighting of him, a great shout would burst out from the kids on the bus and they'd all pile over to the one side, pushing and squabbling and squealing, like piglets to a sow!

The driver didn't even think to stop them, for he liked to see them all so happy, and if the truth were to be coaxed from him, he'd have admitted that he too looked forward to the fun of Robbie's arrival.

'There he is!'

At the top of the hill, where the road poured out of Kincaple Wood, the tiny figure was crouched over the handlebars of his bike, his legs blurring up and down on the pedals!

In the bus, the kids began to chant off the seconds.

One . . . two . . . three . . .

Robbie threw his bike into the corners, leaning hard over, picking his line through the ruts and the stones . . .

Seven . . . eight . . . nine . . .

He'd fitted a wedge of cardboard to the back forks and the spokes rattled across it, roaring like a motor-bike!

Twelve . . . thirteen . . . fourteen . . .

Near to the foot of the road, he banked the bike almost onto its side and skidded along at right angles.

Then, with all the skill and timing of a circus rider, he leapt clear!

The bike hurtled on alone, bucking and bumping before bouncing to rest in the dried-out water-ditch that lined the road.

The count continued while Robbie sprinted on . . .

Nineteen . . . twenty . . . twenty-one . . .

And finally, panting, the little figure scrambled aboard the bus, his eager eyes wide as he listened for his time . . .

Twenty-five . . . twenty-six . . . twenty-seven!

Robbie's arrival! Never more than half a minute, and sometimes, when the wind was strong and from the West, ten seconds less!

The bus wheezed a couple of times and spluttered into life again, then set off along the main road to St Andrews, pausing only once more before it reached town.

At the next road-end to Robbie's — Seafields — collar turned up and hair slicked down, skulking behind a telegraph pole, was Ferrier, known simply and most appropriately as Ferret.

He was tall for a ten-year-old, with a gawky, tight face and darting little eyes that never seemed to find pleasure, but sneered at all they settled on.

Ferret's arrival was not a thing to look forward to.

The whole bus seemed to change when he came slinking aboard. The laughter melted away and the kids found things to study in the fields outside, for sometimes Ferret didn't even like to be looked at.

He swaggered up the aisle, 'accidentally' bumping a few heads with his satchel as he went.

His place at the back of the bus was reserved for him by his two cronies, 'Acne' McCartney, and a pint-sized piece of nastiness called Rankine, whose jaws snatched unceasingly at a

57

wodge of Black Sambo bubble-gum. Even at that early hour of the morning, his upper lip bore a black spiv's moustache, where the bubble had swelled and swelled until, too late, it had sighed and sagged about him!

'Acne' McCartney and Rankine squirmed to the side as their leader approached, leaving the centre of the rear seat free for him to sprawl in.

Ferret was trouble — and always had been.

The Ferriers had arrived at Seafields with all their worldly goods packed into a cattle-float three years before, in the April before the Queen's coronation in 1953.

And right from the start, Ferret had shown exactly what he was made of.

In the June of that year, just a couple of days before the Royal occasion, all the schoolkids had gathered in huge, snaking queues in the playground and had been given Bibles and little, dark-blue tin boxes, with a painting of Her Majesty on the outside and a bar of Cadbury's chocolate on the inside.

All the chocolate had long disappeared by the time the kids were going home at night, but the tin boxes were already prized and treasured possessions, held tightly in little hands.

Ferret's sharp and scheming mind had sized up the situation in a flash and he'd decided that they would be pretty good currency when it came to swopping things!

His plan had been a simple one. He'd taken it into his head to corner the market! And with 'Acne' McCartney gleaming away over one shoulder, and Rankine chewing frantically over the other, Ferret made his move on the bus on the way home.

In most cases, a muttered threat had been enough, but when some opposition had been encountered and there was need of a little persuasion, a quick twist on an arm or a tug at a pigtail had clinched the deal!

And all so smoothly done that the driver, who usually kept an eye on his mirror for signs of trouble, had never seen a thing.

In fact, Ferret would have pulled the whole thing off but for one small obstacle.

Robbie.

His response to the demand was immediate.

The smack of fist on face was like the crack of a whip, and in an instant, the back of the bus became a heaving, tugging, threshing, flailing tangle of bodies!

The driver stood hard on the brakes, then stormed up the aisle and pulled at the heap until it came apart.

As he was hauled to his feet, Ferret rattled away like a tinkers' caravan. From his pockets, fourteen tin boxes were produced.

The driver made him give them all back.

And so was kindled the fire of hatred for Robbie that burned hot inside the heart of Ferret from that day forth.

And more fuel was piled on the following year at the potato holidays, when the Kincaple crop was ready for the lifting.

On the first day of the break, Robbie raced down to the farm with but one thought on his mind – to drive the tractor. One of the men was ill with the shingles and there was a job up for grabs driving up and down the drills while a couple of men filled up the trailer with basketfuls of potatoes, then across with the load to the farm, to the long shed where the dressing was done.

It was a fine job, and much better than being bent double all day long, poking about in the earth with all the muck of the day on your hands and in your nails, and a throb in your back that made standing up a thing to be done in stages!

All the way down the steep hill to the farm, Robbie hoped and hoped. But as he skidded his bike round the corner at the tractor yard, his heart fell like a stone.

Leaning up against the wall, all flashy with coloured tape and stickers, was a drop-handled racing bike. Ferret's bike!

'That makes two of you after the driving job, now!' said Rob Watson, the grieve, a man with a red-raw face and a cap that defied gravity right at the back of his head.

'Ah well, now . . . we'll just have to see . . .'

He frowned, lifted the cap from his head, and ran a hand through his hair.

'We'll just have to see who's the best man for the job . . .'

The two boys watched as the grieve swung up onto the bucket seat of the David Brown tractor and set it roaring into life.

At the far end of the yard was a stone-built loading ramp. Rob Watson took the tractor halfway up the slope of it and killed the engine.

'Now then,' he said when he was back with Robbie and Ferret. 'Who can take it away without it rolling back?'

Ferret moved for the tractor with a rush, but the grieve grabbed him by the collar.

'But before you try, laddie, would you have enough faith in yourself to put your piece-bag in behind the back wheel?'

Ferret stopped in his tracks, his little eyes darting and his tongue flickering over his lips.

'I'll do it with my piece-bag,' offered Robbie. He'd driven the tractor before and was sure of himself.

Ferret's mind was made up in flash.

'It's me first,' he said tightly.

He went over to his bike and, from the back behind the saddle, took out the canvas haversack containing his thermos flask and sandwiches for the day.

Then he placed it in behind the huge rear wheel of the tractor and clambered cockily aboard.

Ferret pulled back on the hand-throttle, roaring and revving the engine.

Black reek rose into the air as he eased his foot up off the clutch . . . slowly . . . slowly . . . he daren't let it roll back or . . . slowly . . . but too eager!

With a jolt, the David Brown took a leap forwards, then the engine stalled and it rolled backwards down the ramp before Ferret could stop it!

There was a crunching sound as the back wheel covered the haversack!

'Ah well,' sighed the grieve. 'It looks like a picking job for you, my lad!'

When it was Robbie's turn to try, he took the tractor away smoothly and gently up the slope from where his piece-bag lay.

'The job's yours,' said Rob Watson, but he had no real need to, for Ferret had conceded, and was walking slowly off towards the field, muttering away to himself as he shook his dripping piece-bag.

At the end of the holidays, Ferret's back ached in a hundred places, and with each and every twinge, he hated Robbie more . . .

Robbie's homeward journey from school was, until one October day in 1956, a thing that he looked forward to.

The bus would shudder to a standstill, the driver would pull back the stiff folding door, and the boy would leap out, free and happy, to be met at the road-end by the old man.

His grandfather was a kind man, a wise man, a gentle man, who knew things, and as the boy wheeled his bicycle up the road, he'd listen in wide-eyed wonder to tales of long ago.

'Did I ever tell you . . .' began the stories, and although Robbie had heard them many times, he never said, for the old man had a way of putting things, a way of waving his stick in the air, a way of stopping to place his hand on the boy's shoulder as he stooped to whisper some special secret – and it was the nearest thing to magic Robbie knew.

Robbie learned a lot from the old man. About the birds that built their nests in the hawthorn hedging on the edge of Kincaple Wood, about the tree that had grown so close to the wire fencing that two of the strands went right through it, and about the grey fur pellets scattered in the grass around the foot of the fence post where the owl took its prey.

The old man knew so much.

But then October . . .

There was a sudden cold spell as the wind swung round, blowing in rain from the North Sea. The old man took a chill and simply, that was the end.

Within a week, with the same peace and dignity that had been in his living, Robbie's grandfather died.

It was a Friday, and still grey with rain. When Robbie left the school bus that night, it was his mother who met him.

She stood at the road end, a lonely figure with a coat held above her head.

And she took the boy under it and held him close . . .

Through the dark and darkening days that followed, the men from the farm came to the cottage to pay their respects, their new-shined boots grating on the gravel path.

Seeing them in sorrow, it was as if Robbie was seeing them for the first time. Will Fenton, Pete Chalmers, Tam Cunningham, Rob Watson – the men from the farm.

Even old Dauve. Strange, quiet old Dauve, who lived for nothing other than the love of his horses.

Robbie had never seen him without his cap before, and the boy noticed how the line of it creased through the greying hair at the back of Dauve's head.

The men stood awkwardly in the front room, ill at ease, some turning their caps through their fingers, speaking in low voices to Robbie's mother. And when they left, they shook hands with Robbie at the door and close to, he smelled the smell of soap and of camphor from the dark serge suits.

And when young Geordie Lee left, he couldn't speak and hurried away into the night.

And then the relatives. Aunts and uncles and cousins Robbie had never seen before.

And the funeral day itself. A fresh wind had risen, bringing the sharpness of winter with it. It stung on the faces like barley stoor at threshing time and it tossed the Reverend Arbuckle's words far and away over the stubble in the fields beyond the kirkyard.

And then the lurching, lowering into the ground and the flop of the cords falling, and then the earth, the dull sound of it as it fell onto the wood . . .

Robbie didn't cry.

Not then, and not after when all the folk were gathered in the cottage. He helped his mother with the tea and the sandwiches and the glasses.

The Reverend Arbuckle stood with his back to the fire, his

thin face drawing in even more as he turned his nose up and away from the tray of whisky glasses offered before him.

There was a quiet as he spread his spindly arms wide then drew them in, clasping his long, bony fingers together at his chest.

'Let us pray . . .' he sang out to the bowed heads before him. 'The Lord giveth and the Lord taketh away. His wisdom is infinite, and inasmuch as we are all but dust, it is as dust that we as sinners all return . . .'

A flicker of something that Robbie could not understand stirred inside him. The boy looked up. The minister's head was tilted up towards the ceiling, his eyes closed tight, the mouth agape as the words came from out of it.

And Robbie didn't understand. Sinners? Why sinners? What did it mean? He bowed his head again as the words spun round in him . . .

'. . . for the Lord our God knows us for our sins and leads us to Him in spite of them. Blessed is the Name of our Lord . . . Amen.'

Even long after the Reverend Arbuckle had taken his sombre leave to drive back up the hill in his black Morris Minor to the high village of Strathkinness, the words still danced in Robbie's head.

And in the minds of others too, he thought. For there was a look on some of the faces that had not been there before. A look that wasn't just grief or sorrow, but was something else. Not anger or hurt even, but a sort of despair. Robbie couldn't understand it, but he could see that it was there for all that.

But slowly, slowly, like a sun rising above fields of rime, warming, warming, warming, there crept in a change as the talk turned to thoughts of the old man. It seemed as if everyone had a tale to tell.

Of the dignity that had always seemed to be a part of him. Of the quiet way he had with himself and with others. Of his love, and of his wisdom.

And then it was Rob Watson, draining his glass, then wiping the back of his hand across his mouth. He smiled and shook his head in pleasures remembered.

'Do you mind that time with Lady Gibson?' he began, and straightaway, a ripple like a warm gust whispering through a field of wheat spread across the room.

It was a well remembered story.

'She'd moved into that cottage near Monksholm from some big estate up North. Brought all her airs and graces with her – but no staff, and little money folks said at the time.

'So she was after a gardener, and got chackin' to the old man, wondering if he'd turn over the wee bit ground for her and maybe put in a few vegetables.

'So he says he'd give it a bit of thought and she says the job's his for the taking – providing, of course, his references were to her satisfaction. It was just her gentry way of speaking, you understand.'

Rob Watson broke off to take a gulp from a fresh glass of whisky. He wiped at his mouth again, eyes fair shining with the story.

'Well, the old lad had his bit of a thought, and decided she could do with his help so up he goes, carrying his spade under one arm, and with a muckle cardboard box under the other.

'And when she came to his knock on the door, he just smiled thon smile of his, and he tips up the box. And onto the grass pours this pile of vegetables – carrots, and leeks, and neeps and onions. And a' grown to perfection in the wee bit patch outside this very room we're standing in.

' "My references" was all that he said. Then he got on wi' the diggin'!'

The room was warmer now, and Robbie left it, strangely happy, but wanting to be alone, on his own somewhere.

He went to the shed. To the split kindling and the thick smell of fresh sawn logs.

Hanging from hooks on the ceiling were strings of onions, plaited bunches, hanging heavy and still, so still.

And leaning against the wall, the old man's spade. Draped on the handle, his jacket.

Slowly, dreaming almost, Robbie reached for it, then held it close to him, and closer and closer and tighter to him. And the friendly, familiar smells of pipe tobacco and peppermints seemed to soak right into him.

And he buried his face deep into the jacket, and the tears came sweetly from him.

When Robbie went back to school, he never raced his bike down the rough road, and the kids, sensing the sorrow in him, chanted out no time.

He sat silently at the window, looking out at the fields, scarcely seeing the change in them as the early ploughs turned the stubble all to brown.

No one spoke to him and he spoke to no one, for his thoughts and his solitude were all he wanted.

All the kids on the bus knew this and felt it. All of them, that is, except for one.

Ferret.

There was no room in him for anything but evil, and it wasn't long after Robbie was back that he saw his chance and took it . . .

It happened on a day when, aboard the bus, greeted by a chorus of hissing from rows of seemingly innocent faces, came Inspector Duff – a beaky faced little man with a peaked cap and a long, dark-blue gaberdine trenchcoat, which he wore fully buttoned up in all weathers.

He was a nervous man and he sniffed a lot and the kids all took to sniffing back – which just made him worse.

At the beginning of each term, all the children on the bus were issued with season tickets and little plastic folders to keep them in – and it was Inspector Duff's duty to arrive unannounced and see to it that all was in order.

He threaded his way up the aisle, checking the passes, nodding and sniffing, nodding and sniffing, nodding and sniffing.

But when he came to Robbie, he stopped.

No ticket!

The boy had to go through all of his pockets twice and one of them three times before it turned up, all crumpled and grubby like it had been cawed through the swede-mangle!

On the wooden-slatted seat beside him lay the contents of Robbie's pockets. Three handkerchiefs, some pencils, a badge with an eagle on it, a couple of toffees, a penny that a train had gone over – and a photograph of his grandfather, kept neatly in the little plastic folder he'd been given for his season ticket!

It was a grand photograph, taken on an autumn day last year when the old man and his traction engine had hauled a Hawker Hunter out of the mud on the Eden Estuary.

But Inspector Duff could not have cared less about the old man's triumph!

'Careless! Untidy! Downright slovenly!' rang out his voice on the bus, with of course, the sniffing in between!

And Ferret, leering over the seat behind Robbie grinned wider and wider and wider.

In the confusion, the photograph fell through the slats onto the floor.

When it turned up later, someone had taken a pen and had added a scar and crossed the eyes.

Ferret never stopped smiling all the way to school.

And he was still leering away at night, and as if to try to rub salt into the wound, he began a session of his unique brand of bragging.

Like a cockerel on a dung-heap, he crowed all the way home from his perch at the back of the bus. And all aimed at getting to Robbie.

It was Seafields this and Seafields that. How their new combine harvester could do half a field by the time the Kincaple binders had been threaded up with twine.

Robbie at first tried to ignore it, but there was little chance of that.

How the Seafield bull had sired a hundred more calves than that clapped-out bag-of-bones Kincaple had!

Robbie felt the anger swell inside him. He gripped the seat in front of him, his knuckles white, his jaw set.

And how the blue Seafields Fordson Major tractors were so much better than the two tinny red David Browns that Kincaple had!

66

'Fordies! Fordies! Fordies!' sang Ferret and his pair of pals.

Then, suddenly, and with no real feeling of actually getting up, Robbie found himself on his feet.

'David Browns,' was all he said.

There was a stunned silence in the bus.

'Fordies,' said Ferret, tight like.

'David Browns.'

'Fordies.'

The words stotted like a ball back and forwards between them.

'Blues,' said Ferret.

'Reds,' said Robbie, matching him.

Then there followed a typical piece of Ferret thinking. He declared that seeing as there were more blue cars than red ones on the road, blue was more popular than red, therefore blue Fordies were better than red David Browns – so there!

Robbie was in too deep to back out, and his reply was almost automatic. He said red was more popular so David Browns were best – so there, yourself!

'Blue,' said Ferret.

'Red,' said Robbie.

And so, from a silly, meaningless, schoolboy argument, the idea of a competition was born!

They decided that, the next day, on the way to school in the morning and on the way home again at night, they'd look at all the cars on the road. Robbie would get a point for all the red ones, and Ferret a point for all the blues.

There were to be no prizes, but at the same time, both boys knew that everything was at stake – pride, prestige, self respect, everything that really mattered.

And what a morning it was!

The whole busload of kids had their noses pressed so hard up against the windows that the glass all misted up and they had to wipe it clear with their cuffs every few minutes! And when Ferret came swaggering aboard, the competition had begun.

It was even enough to begin with. First a red car, then a long lull, then a blue and then another red.

But then, on the outskirts of St Andrews, there came a disaster for Robbie. A milk-float from the local dairy – as blue as blue could be!

'Blue!' squealed Ferret in ecstasy.

Robbie said that they shouldn't count, but Ferret and his pals howled him down and pretty soon it was cheers for anything blue with wheels! And when they trooped off the bus at the school gates, the score stood at 6 blues – and only 3 reds!

Robbie was last off the bus, his schoolbag bouncing down the steps as he trailed it by the length of its strap.

And he was last on at night, too, and after a day's jeering and taunting and jibing by Ferret and Rankine and 'Acne' McCartney, his eyes were still full and red rubbed.

They'd stalked him all day, in the classrooms, in the playground, in the dinner hut – pushing and poking and prodding until it had all been too much and the tears had come bursting through.

The driver gave Robbie a cheering grin as he went by. But there was no sign of mercy from Ferret.

He was already bouncing up and down at the window. The competition had to go on!

And straightaway, they passed a couple of blue cars – 8–3!

But then Robbie's luck seemed to take a turn for the better as three red cars in a row passed by.

8–6!

Then another red car! But it was followed closely by a blue one, and then came·another milk-float!

Ferret shrieked away, cackling like a crow, and banging his fists together.

The driver glanced up in his mirror as the bus stood ticking over, waiting for a gap in the stream of traffic that poured through the West Port, the ancient city gateway in the heart of St Andrews.

He saw Robbie, and he could see that the tears were pretty close again.

The boy needed a break. A bit of good luck in his life for a change. But with the score standing at 10–7 against him, it was more than a break he needed, it was a miracle!

And then, quite simply, it happened.

The driver gave a sudden chuckle to himself, then he pulled and fed the steering wheel through his hands.

With a lurch, the schoolbus swung round and through the West Port! Ferret was on his feet in a flash!

'Hey, driver! You've gone the wrong way! You've gone right by mistake!'

The driver smiled. It was no mistake – merely a small detour.

The bus chugged slowly along the length of South Street, along towards the Post Office. And there, lined up in a long row was a whole fleet of pillar-box red, Post Office vans!

The driver stopped the bus, right in the middle of South Street. He leaned back in his seat and listened to the count soaring!

The next morning, Robbie began racing down the road again, and to a great roar from all the kids on the school bus, he took three whole seconds off his record!

THE TINKS

THE RAINBOW began in the east, shining from out of the mirk that hung over the countryside.

It swung big and bright and bold against the slate sky, in a brilliant arc, well above the swell of farmland known as Monksholm and the faint grey outline of Strathkinness beyond.

From the cart, the boy followed the curve, fair taken with the thing, with the colours and the great sweep of it all the way over above them and then down.

It seemed to Robbie that it plunged right into Kincaple Den!

Beside him, twitching at the reins that jiggled back along the flanks of the horse was Dauve, his cap unstudded and pulled hard down, and the collar of his vast, black overcoat reaching up toward it.

Dauve had no time for the rainbow, he saw only the steady swing of Punch, the Clydesdale, in between the trams. And he heard nothing of the land about him, the soaking, dripping land, the peewit and the curlew – he heard only the jingle of the harness, the rub of the great spoked wheels, and the dull thud-thuddings of the hooves into the softened earth.

'Do you think they'll be there, Dauve?' asked Robbie. 'The tinks – do you think they'll be in the Den wood yet?'

Dauve said not a word, but made a click-click sound and sent a ripple along the lengths of rein as Punch checked before splashing into the stillness of a long, grey pool of water.

He looked at the flecks of mud that splattered up onto the horse and its harness. It would all have to be cleaned – but not that he minded for it was a job that he loved, cleaning the horse and its harness, late into the night when the moths whirred and danced around the light of the oil-lamps in the stable.

Always the last to leave was Dauve. When the others had finished and were off for home with the idea growing of having a quick bit tea then striding up the hills to the Corner Bar in Strathkinness, Dauve was still there, sitting alone on the straw bales in the corner of the stable.

And often, when he'd no mind to be in his bothy on his own, he'd still be there long hours after, just rubbing at the brass, huffing on it, coaxing the shine deeper and deeper into it.

And he'd hear the men trailing back down the road, singing and roaring each louder than the other, and then their women-folk yelling and yowling at the doorsteps and he'd shake his head at the daftness of it all then get on with the shining.

But, man, it was worth it. And not just for the certificates and rosettes he'd won at shows and had pinned to the mirror above the mantelpiece.

No, there was more to it than that.

His harness sparkled sharper than any other horseman's, catching the light and keeping it, the gleaming brass and the dull, dark leather, as black as the back of the coalshed door.

And when he went out through the village of Kincaple with his pair, Punch and Jeck, Dauve was fair lifted to see the folks stop whatever it was that they were doing, and poke and nudge at each other, and point and look up in awe as the horses jingled by, all plaited up and combed, shining and tinkling and gleaming, and the great polished hooves the colour of new-run honey, thudding down onto the road and fair making it tremble.

It was all Dauve had . . . but it was all he ever wanted.

'That was some storm, though,' tried Robbie again on the cart.

There was still no reply.

But it had been some storm. For nearly a week, there hadn't been a break to the scream of the west wind and the rattle of the driven rain. And now, it was as if the whole country-side had been trampled on.

The battered stacks, the gaps in the roofs where the red pantiles had been snatched clean away, and the big, tar-painted door of the granary, left swinging on a single buckled hinge after the wind had all but clawed it off.

In the woods around the village, trees that had taken score upon score of years to shoot and swell and reach, had been snapped in an instant, and the ditches that lined the roads were full and roaring with the weight of clay-clouded water.

'There'll be no lifting for a while yet,' said Robbie, looking over the stone dyke into the flooded potato field beyond. More than half the drills were under water, and scores of seabirds had scuttled up from the mudflats on the Eden estuary to feed and splash and squabble in new surroundings.

Dauve still said nothing, just coaxed the horse along.

The storm meant but one thing to him, the work that it had caused. The old quarry hole at the top of the Den Wood had filled and swelled over, washing away the road that had skirted it.

It would need a good few cartloads of stones to give it new bottoming – a mucky job, and a back-breaking one, forbye.

Just then, the cart lurched over the last rise before the farm track rolled down to meet the top of the Den Wood.

And then Robbie saw it!

A thin smear of wood smoke, white against the grey sky, faint and sparse as it trickled up through the trees, but there, nonetheless.

'The tinks!' cried Robbie. 'The tinks have come!'

Dauve looked up from below the peak of his cap, and for the first time that morning, he spoke to someone other than his horses.

'Damn tinks,' he muttered. And again, 'Damn tinks.'

It was no secret that Dauve, like many folk in the village, hated the tinks. He'd never given reason, perhaps it was because of the way some of them were supposed to mistreat their horses, Robbie wasn't sure.

But of one thing he was certain, Dauve's dislike of the tinks was a deep-running thing.

'I'll give them your regards, will I?' yelled Robbie as he

vaulted over the side board of the cart. 'Thanks for the lift, Dauve!'

His laughter scurried into the wood after him.

Dauve made a click-click sound, and shook at the reins.

Kincaple Den was a mile or so long, a great split in the earth, steep-sided and thick with trees and bushes and tangled undergrowth.

A stream tumbled out of the old quarry hole at the top end, then cut its way deeper and deeper into the Den, down and down towards the flat marshlands of the Eden estuary at Guardbridge.

It was of no use at all as farmland, but it made a fine walk for folks on the Sabbath after the kirk, especially in the autumn, when the path that wound down through the trees was lined with bramble bushes, thick and heavy with berries.

There were none sweeter in all the countryside, and many a couple all toffed up in their Sunday best at the top end of the Den, were ripped and torn and well-stained with bramble juice by the time they reached the foot!

But it was worth it for the taste. Well worth it for the taste . . .

It was in the late autumn that the tinks came, at the back end of the year when the potato harvest was ready for the lifting. They came from the North, from beyond the Tay, from the Carse of Gowrie berryfields, and for them, Kincaple was the next spoke on the wheel that turned never-ending through the seasons.

They came with a pony, a sad-eyed, chestnut and white little thing that pulled at a cart laden high with all that the tinks owned – and a lot that they didn't own, as some folks said.

About eight of them there were, sometimes less, led by an old man who walked at the pony's head while the others trailed behind.

And they were hardy, all of them, even the womenfolk, one of whom had walked all the way with an infant wrapped in close to her breast. She would work, too, just the same as the rest of them, with the baby happed up in a blanket in between the drills, and being fed and shifted every now and then throughout the length of the long, hard days.

But there was no work just now. Nor would there be for a while, until the fields had dried enough for the diggers and carts to travel across them without sinking right up to the axles in the tight squeeze of the clay ground.

In a way, Robbie was glad.

He was near to the camp, now, near the hollow in the Den where the tinks pitched their tent. He could just make out the shape of it, like an upturned boat, a green tarpaulin stretched over a tied framework of birch branches.

The pony was hobbled nearby, and didn't hear him as it snuffled in among the mast at the roots of a beech tree.

Robbie was closer now. The smoke was sharp in his nostrils, and he could hear the muted murmur of voices from within the tent. There was a scrap of a mongrel dog tied to a length of rope, but it hadn't noticed him, being too intent on toying with a ball made out of a rabbit skin.

Robbie's heartbeat quickened and his mouth went dry as he wondered to himself just how close he could get!

He edged forward, creeping like an Indian brave. He scampered to the cover of the beech tree beside the pony, his heart drumming now.

He peeped round from the tree, planning his next move.

And then, without sound or warning, the hands were on him! From behind, strong hands at his neck!

Instinctively, Robbie ducked down, reaching up behind him, grabbing for the arms. He clawed for them, got a firm grip, then pulled the weight up and over his shoulder!

A body arched over his, through the air, and landed, agile as a cat on the ground in front of him. It was a young tinker lad, about the same age as Robbie, and dark and strong.

His eyes stared hard at Robbie, the hands out and ready, ready to spring in close and grip again. Robbie mirrored his movements, watching him closely, waiting, matching, circling.

Twice the young tink lad made to lunge forwards, but darted back like a weasel when he saw that Robbie had the move covered. And still they circled, each stalking the other.

And then suddenly, the game was ended. Each at the same

time, they straightened up, hands down and relaxed, smiling first and then laughing.

'McPhee,' grinned Robbie. 'I was beginning to think you weren't coming this year.'

'No fear,' said McPhee.

And with that, their friendship was rekindled.

The two boys had first met at the potato lifting a couple of years before, their bits being together at the top end of the drill.

To begin with, it wasn't so much a friendship as a conspiracy that had drawn them together, for late in the afternoon, when their backs were fair throbbing and their fingers aching where the earth had packed in behind their nails, they'd noticed the big boulder lying in the long grass at the edge of the field.

The same dark thought had occurred to them both at the very same instant!

Sabotage!

As soon as the digger had passed by, they tore into their bits with renewed effort, filling a couple of wire baskets each in double quick time.

When they were done and the machine was over the brow at the bottom end of the run, they struggled with the stone together, rolling it over and over, for it was too heavy to lift.

With lightning speed, they scraped out a hole from the next drill and tumbled the stone into it, then happed it over, as neat as you like.

And not a moment too soon, for they'd just finished patting the drill into shape when the tractor and digger came bouncing up the field, ready for another run.

Robbie and McPhee watched, biting at their lips, as the tractor turned beside them, lined up, then moved forward with the digger's flailing arms birling, birling, birling.

There was an almighty clatter as metal struck onto stone! A chain-drive snapped and bits of the digger spun into the air!

A great cheer soared up from the whole squad as Rob Watson the grieve strode up the field to join the driver. The pair of them stood beside the stricken digger with their caps off, scratching at their heads, wondering how in heaven's name such a muckle boulder had not been seen and removed at the planting.

Robbie and McPhee hardly dared to look at each other, but concentrated on keeping their eyes wide and the innocent look on their faces for as long as they could.

With a sigh, Rob Watson took a great kick at the digger and declared, in a rather colourful fashion, that the machine was well and truly finished for the day!

And with that, Robbie and McPhee's friendship was well and truly started.

That year, and the following, they spent as much of their free time as they could together – playing, exploring, capering, and sometimes, getting into mischief just for the ripples of sheer pleasure that it gave them!

Like the time one piece-break, when they'd been in the granary looking for mice. On the floor, near some sacks of feed, they'd come across the cattleman's working boots, discarded after he'd changed to go indoors for his break.

With two six-inch nails, they'd fixed them to the wooden floorboards . . .

A short time later, after his piece, the poor man had changed back into them, laced them up – and had taken a terrible tumble, banging his knees, chest and chin all at one and the same time!

They heard the roaring and ran . . .

And another time, when there were three Irish labourers in the wooden caravan the shepherd used at lambing time. They'd been hired on piece-work to mend some gaps in the drystone dykes up near Strathkinness, but one morning, late on, there was neither sight nor sound of any of them.

The grieve had gone and battered his huge fist on the door until they'd appeared, red-eyed and blinking at the daylight – and muttering about it being still dark.

The black paint on the windows was still wet to the touch . . .

And, of course, there was the occasion when the Reverend

76

Arbuckle from the Parish of Strathkinness had been down in the village.

He'd driven his black Morris Minor all the way back to his church blissfully unaware of the fact that he was trailing a pair of big Aggie Cunningham's satin bloomers, fresh pinched from her washing line and filled out in the wind behind his car like a Spanish galleon in full sail – and him on his way to a kirk session meeting, too, with all the council in attendance!

But it wasn't all fun and capering.

For McPhee was a tink, and tinks were not to be trusted. They were a sleekit set and would steal anything, or so folks said.

It was a funny thing though, thought Robbie, that for most of the year, eggs would go missing – even hens – to the fox or the rat or the weasel. It happened, it was just the way of things.

For most of the year, folks never paid too much heed – but if it happened during one of the few weeks when the tinks were camping in the Den, then it was them that got the blame.

They weren't liked. And some of the older womenfolk in the village had tales of how a tink could give a certain look and nothing but bad luck would follow – even a death, some said.

And then there was old Dauve. The very mention of their name was enough to make him spit.

But to Robbie, McPhee wasn't a tink. He was different. He was a friend.

It was McPhee last year who'd said nothing to Robbie about his grandfather, even although he knew that he'd died. And Robbie had sensed this, and was glad of his consideration.

And it was McPhee last year who'd taught him how to guddle for trout down where the burn was wider at the foot of the Den. He'd shown him how to lie along the bank and ease his arm in below the water, searching, searching. And then the soft, cold belly of the fish lying in the current, and tickling, tickling, tickling at it. Gently stroking . . . gently . . . gently . . . then round the gills and up and out of the water

77

and onto the banking, with the thing wriggling and gasping on the grass!

There was nothing better in all the world, cleaning it there and then, threading it onto a peeled bit stick and cooking it fresh above a smoking wood fire.

But there would be no tickling for trout this year, for the stream was swollen high, and in every part of the Den Wood, they could hear the water grumbling and rumbling like rolls of thunder.

The two boys sat facing each other astride a fallen silver birch tree, kicking their legs idly, just enjoying the feel of the weight of their boots.

'I'm reading a fine like book just now,' said Robbie. 'In my bed at night with a torch.'

'Can you read?' asked McPhee. 'The words and all that – can you read them?'

'Aye, I can read,' said Robbie, a bit puzzled. 'Why? Can you not, like?'

McPhee shrugged, took out his knife, and poked the point of it into the bark of the tree.

'Well . . . sort of . . . a wee bit . . .' Then, 'No, I canny read.' He concentrated hard on the knife.

'I'll teach you if you want,' offered Robbie.

McPhee shrugged again. He was flushed, and his mouth had taken a sort of tight look as he spoke.

'Aye . . . you can do that,' he said casual like. 'One of these days . . .'

'Aye, one of these days,' agreed Robbie, leaving it at that. Then he too got out his knife.

'And what was this fine book of yours about anyway?' asked McPhee later, after a silence had stretched between them.

'Geronimo – leader of the Apache nation. A real Indian!'

'Like Sitting Bull?' asked McPhee.

'Aye – except better. Geronimo once led all his braves right through a soldiers' camp. Sneaked right through they did, and not a soul heard them!'

McPhee gave a bit snort. There was still a tightness about him.

78

'Mind you, sneaking up's pretty easy.'

'Bet you couldn't have done it!' retorted Robbie.

McPhee sniffed. 'I don't know about that,' he said. 'I'm pretty good, you know.'

'Away, man,' said Robbie. 'You couldn't do that.'

'Could,' said McPhee, thrawn-like.

Robbie grinned, then thought for a while, licking his tongue back and forwards along his lower lip.

'All right,' he said at length. 'You can show me just how good you are at sneaking up. Old Dauve's working up on the quarry road today – let's see you sneaking up on him!'

McPhee took to the challenge immediately. His jaw had a determined jut to it.

'And does he have his horse with him?' he asked, sort of matter-of-fact like.

Robbie nodded.

'Right,' said McPhee. 'I'll tell you what I'll do.' He held his knife up, narrowed his eyes to slits, and stroked his thumb across the blade. 'I'll sneak up, nick a couple of hairs out of his horse's tail and old Dauve won't even know I've been near him!'

Robbie blew out a long, low whistle. 'Now that's what I'd call sneaking up!'

The pair of them gave a giggle, then swung down from the tree.

'C'mon, Geronimo,' said Robbie. 'Let's go!'

Dauve had carted three loads of stones and rubble and tipped them onto the bare track that skirted the quarry – and there was hardly anything to show for all the sweat. The flood-water had come rushing down the road, sweeping and scraping all the surface from it. It would take him all that day, and the next one, too, by the look of it.

He gave a quick flick at the reins and Punch moved on, his great ironed hooves slithering on the new-laid bottoming as he took the strain of another load up the slope.

Dauve shook his head, and a small smile of admiration came

79

to his lips. It never failed to amaze him to see the strength of a horse. Punch's flanks rippled as he pushed into his collar, all his weight pressing forward, forward as the cart lurched up the incline.

And then it happened!

A great slab of the ground simply tilted, broke away, and tipped into the waters of the quarry! For a moment, the cart was motionless – but then slowly, eerily, like a great tree falling, it swung round.

Dauve was flung clear as the cart slewed over the edge of the quarry! He fell heavily, and the breath was thumped from his body.

Punch slithered backwards, pulled by the great weight of stones in the cart. His hooves slithered in the muck, trying to find grip, to find some solid ground from which to push. But there was nothing – and back and back and back he was hauled!

The great horse was on his knees now, thrashing with his hind legs. Clouds of steam plumed from his mouth and nostrils as he heaved and struggled against the weight. Surely, surely his heart would burst!

Dauve stirred, made to move towards the stricken horse, but couldn't. His body ached and had no strength in it.

'My God! No – No!' he gasped, his fingers stretched, trembling towards the beast. They dug and clawed into the clay ground.

Punch's eyes rolled white and wild and his head tossed and plunged as his screams filled the air!

Dauve crawled forward, each movement sending stabs of agony through him. But he had to do something . . . he had to do something . . .

And then the boy was there!

The dark-haired, tinker boy! With one vault, McPhee was on the Clydesdale's broad back. With his knife, he hacked at the leather strapping at the top of the horse's collar.

But there was no time, surely! The cart was in the water now, and already the horse's hind legs were thrashing out at the chill grip. Any second now and the cart would be right over the edge, dragging the horse down and down and down . . .

But still McPhee hacked at the strip of leather between the hames in front of the collar.

And suddenly, it gave! The shafts of the cart dropped. There was only one strap now . . . only one . . .

Again the knife slashed at the leather. But this strap was thicker.

Robbie was beside Dauve now, and the old man clung to him as they watched.

The water was up to the horse's back nearly, and McPhee's hands were working below the surface.

'Get clear, laddie!' roared Dauve. 'Save yourself! You'll never do it!'

But he did!

The leather band gave and the cart fell over backwards. It plunged out of sight, down and down into the dark waters in a great gurgle of froth and bubbles.

Punch, free now of the load, scrambled and scraped for grip at the edge of the quarry. His forelegs found some solid ground, and with an almighty effort that only desperation could summon, he hauled himself up and out with McPhee clinging to his neck.

The great horse lurched up the banking, then, exhausted, sank to its knees on the ground. McPhee crouched beside the horse, blowing gently into the nostrils to calm him until he was strong enough to stand.

And all the while, Dauve sat with his head buried into his hands, his back shuddering as he sobbed.

From that weekend onwards, whenever the tinks were in the Den, a box was left on a flat boulder near the path at the top end.

In it would be vegetables, or eggs, sometimes a coat or a blanket.

No one ever said where they came from.

THE WILD GEESE

THE LANDS OF KINCAPLE flowed gently from the high
grounds of Strathkinness, down and down in a run of green and
gradual undulations.

The farm itself, a clutter of old, sandstone buildings, had
been built into the slope of the last of the waves of hills, then
below it, the ground spread itself flat and wide and fertile, right
down to the marshlands that skirted the River Eden.

It was in one of the bottom fields, the one that was nearest
to the fringes of whispering reeds and rushes, that Robbie and
McPhee built the hide.

They'd worked well that Sunday, trailing long branches down
from the Den Wood across the stubble field. It was hard
and heavy going, and the field was wet with late October
dampness.

Their leather boots were soaked and heavy, but they'd long
since stopped caring about that.

The plan! That was all that mattered! That was all they
thought about . . .

They rammed the bigger branches on end into the clay
ground, in a rough circle just big enough to hold the pair of
them. Then, in between the main branches, they threaded
smaller ones, and reeds and clumps of grass, leaving but a small
entrance gap to wriggle into, and a couple of little slits to peep
out of!

All morning it took them, and well into the afternoon. But
it was worth it. The hide was near perfect.

'Can you see in?' called Robbie in a coarse whisper to
McPhee, who stood outside.

'Not a sign of you!' came the tinker boy's hushed reply.

It was strange them whispering, for the whole field was

empty but for the pair of them, and the nearest houses were across the estuary in Guardbridge, over a mile away!

But dark deeds were afoot, and secrecy was all important.

'What about the grain?' whispered McPhee.

'There's a bin in the stables with loads of the stuff,' said Robbie. 'I'll get a bagful on my way back.'

'And the . . . the . . .' McPhee paused to look around before he dared say the word. His dark eyes shone with the devilment. 'And the whisky?'

Robbie grinned.

'My mother has some in the press. I'll get it tonight.'

'So it's tonight then?' asked McPhee.

Robbie looked up at the pale, silver sky. There was no cloud and already a big moon hung up in the east, shining like a half-crown.

'There'll be loads of light tonight. We'll see them fine!'

And so it was arranged.

The plan they'd worked out at the potato picking through the week was ready to be put to the test.

They'd been taking their break together, lying on their backs in the drills in the field up by the Den Wood when they'd come swinging over – the geese!

'It'd be a fine thing getting a couple of them,' Robbie had said, aiming and firing both barrels of an imaginary twelve-bore at the leading bird.

They'd watched the skein circle, lower and lower, cautious, looking out for any sign of danger. Round they went, and again in a wide sweep, but lower and lower all the time. Then, together, the flock had settled down into the barley stubble of the bottom field.

'We'd need some sort of a hide,' McPhee had said. 'Then we could sit in it at night and wait until they were close –'

'And grab them!' Robbie had cried. 'But . . . but they'd rise before we were near . . .'

There was a long silence as they both let the thoughts race through their minds.

'But what if we doped them, somehow,' Robbie had said. 'Then they'd be that bit slower in taking off . . .'

'Aye,' McPhee had said. 'But what could we dope them with . . . ?'

The last pieces of the plan had fallen neatly into place.

And now they were ready to test it.

'I'll give you a hoot about midnight,' Robbie said as the two boys reached the top corner of the field at the foot of the Den Wood. And with no more than that, they parted. McPhee heading for his tinker's camp in the hollow halfway up the Den, and Robbie back to the stone cottage in the village of Kincaple.

But first through the farm. He had some grain to get.

Robbie slipped quiet as a cat through the farmyard, keeping his body close to the walls, edging up to corners, peeping round then scampering across the open spaces until he was at the stables.

He put his weight against the sliding door, hoping, hoping that the cast-iron wheels wouldn't squeak on the runners and give him away. But no sound came, and when the gap was a few inches wide, he squeezed inside, hauling it quietly closed behind him.

All the horses were in their stalls. Summer days had withered into autumn and were fallen and were gone, days when the Clydesdales had spent their free hours turned loose in the lush, green park at the back of the farm. Days of capering and cantering, and nuzzling friendly like at each other's shoulders where the collars had pressed hard onto them when they'd been toiling through the long hours.

But the grass had lost its sweetness, and the horses had been moved inside, to the warmth of the deep straw, and the rich clover flavour of the hay in the mangers.

Two of the horses tossed their heads to see who the intruder was, but just for a moment, then it was back to tugging at a clump of hay and squeezing the sweet juices from it.

Robbie moved quietly down to the huge bins at the far end of the stable. He tugged at the lid, heaved it open, then dipped his hand inside. It was crushed oats . . . just what he was after!

There was a sack lying near and he picked it up, shaking the stoor from it in a great cloud. The dust tickled at his nose but he fought off the sneeze. No one must find him!

Then he delved a scoop into the bin and poured a cascade of oats into the open mouth of the sack. Then again. And again.

As he dipped in for the fourth time, the voice came from behind him!

'And just what do you think you're up to, laddie?'

Robbie whirled and the scoop flew out of his hand, clattering to the floor and birling on the stone as he gaped, eyes wide, heart hammering.

From out of the end stall, from out of the shadows, came Dauve. Old Dauve, the strange quiet horseman who spent nearly every hour he had in the company of his pair of Clydesdales.

'Well, laddie – have you lost your tongue?'

Robbie's head reeled. The plan – he mustn't reveal the plan!

'It's for – it's for the hens!' he stammered out. 'We've got nothing to feed them on. Can I – can I take a wee bagful?'

Dauve was close now, and his grey eyes stared hard at Robbie. They narrowed. For a long minute, Dauve said nothing. Then he made a sort of snorting noise and nodded.

'Aye, I suppose you can.'

Relief washed through Robbie, and he made to dash off with his plunder, but Dauve plucked the sack from his hand.

'But you'll have to earn this! You'll have to give me a hand with the horses.'

Kincaple Farm had four pairs of Clydesdale horses, and none looked better than Punch and Jeck, the two that old Dauve worked.

Their coats had more of a sheen, their harness more of a shine, and they even appeared to move better, with a self assured swing to their walk that seemed to speak of the respect they had for the man.

It was a handsome sight seeing Dauve at the close of the day, sitting sideways up on Jeck with Punch in right behind, fair full of themselves, a real team and matched just right for each other.

He was a strange sort, dour and sullen, keeping himself to himself. He lived alone in a cramped little bothy in the village, but folks said it was more in the way of being a holiday home for Dauve, and that his real home was down in the stables for it was there that he spent most of his time, grooming his horses, talking to them, and polishing at the brass and leather of the harnesses.

Dauve handed Robbie a rope-handled, wooden bucket.

'You can fill that up with fine sawdust for me,' he said. 'And make sure it's dry stuff, mind!'

Robbie scurried round to the saw bench. The men had been making fence-stabs, and beneath the jagged, circular blade was a great mound of white sawdust. The boy delved the bucket into it and filled it to the brim.

When he returned to the stable, Dauve was at his horses. He was bathing their feet, washing the great plumed hooves. When he'd finished, he took handfuls of the sawdust and rubbed it into the long hair, working it right in. Then he brushed it all out and combed each foot in turn.

'What do you do that for?' asked Robbie.

'It dries them,' answered Dauve, picking up each hoof in turn to inspect the hair and the shoe. 'The sawdust dries the hair. Makes a grand like job.'

Dauve picked at a hoof, coaxing out a stone.

'It's all a question of care,' he said. 'You mind that when you're older and you're working a pair of horse for yourself.'

Robbie grinned.

'But it'll not be horse then, Dauve. The farm'll be all tractors by that time.'

Dauve straightened up and for a moment, a strange look seemed to come on him – a far away look, either remembering days gone by or imagining days yet to come. Robbie wasn't sure.

Then Dauve snatched up Robbie's bag of oats and tossed it to him.

'Get away with you,' was all he said.

When he reached his cottage, Robbie didn't go in straight away. Instead, he went into the wash-house next door. He took a pail and poured the crushed oats into it, then hid it behind the fat, black boiler.

Then he gave his boots a quick brush with the broom, stuck his hands deep into his pockets and whistled as he sauntered, all innocent like, round the corner and home.

'And just where on earth have you been?' His mother's words rattled like hail as she met him at the door. 'Nothing inside your belly since breakfast! You'll have been with that McPhee, I'll bet – and up to some mischief or other!'

Robbie made his eyes go wide, and looked up at his mother.

'I've been helping Dauve, Mum,' he said. 'He wanted a hand with his horses.'

Robbie's mother looked hard at him for a moment.

'I'd have thought Dauve was able to look after his horses just fine without your assistance!'

But then, with a light skelp at his head, she smiled.

'Come on,' she said. 'There's some stewed hare in the oven – you're bound to be starving.'

Seconds later, the dish was out of the oven at the side of the fire, and before him, hot and steaming up into his face.

Robbie drew the sweet smell deep inside him, savouring the mouth-watering scent of it all.

'There's nothing to beat stewed hare, Mum,' he said, dipping a chunk of bread into the rich gravy. 'Except maybe,' he added, 'a nice roast goose.'

Robbie smiled a secret little smile to himself.

After he'd shut away the hens for the night, and filled up with sticks and coal, and done all the rest of his chores, Robbie put the final stages of his plan into action.

His mother was sitting by the fire in the living-room, darning a new heel into a sock. She looked up over the top of her spectacles as the boy came through from the kitchen and her eyes opened wide with surprise.

'I've made you some tea!' Robbie announced, pouring what he'd spilt in the saucer back into the cup.

His mother beamed into a smile and shook her head in amazement.

'My, Robbie,' she exclaimed, putting her darning to one side. 'How lovely!'

'It's my pleasure, Mum,' declared Robbie grandly.

He sat by the fender, watching his mother sip at the brew. There was sugar in it – she took none – and the water hadn't been brought fully to the boil, giving it a coarse, raw sort of taste that fair scraped at the palate. But his mother said nothing, just sipped at it with a look of pleasure and contentment on her.

'Would you like some more?' Robbie asked when the last of it was gone. His mother shook her head – but not too much.

'No thank you, Robbie – that was just lovely.'

'Well, you bide where you are, Mum, and I'll wash the cup for you.'

And with that, the boy left, closing the door behind him and just missing the smile that tugged at the corners of his mother's mouth.

In the kitchen, Robbie rushed into action.

He eased open the press door and there it was – the whisky bottle! He carried it carefully in two hands over to the table, eased off the cork, and poured its entire contents into a jug.

Then he took the teapot and at the sink, half filled up the empty bottle with tea. Then he topped it up with water until the colour was just right, and rammed the cork back in.

His hands trembled as he slid the whisky bottle back to its place on the shelf in the press.

After that, he took the torch, let himself silently out of the kitchen door, and hurried as much as he dared with the full jug of whisky.

In the wash-house, he poured the whisky into the bucket of crushed oats and was back in the kitchen in seconds, whistling loudly and rattling at the cup and saucer in the sink.

Unaware of it all, his mother still sat darning in the living-room, sucking at a peppermint, trying to rid her palate of the taste of the tea.

As he lay in bed that night, Robbie's heart seemed to pound away inside him like the mill at threshing time!

The plan! The plan! The plan! His head fairly thundered with the thought of it.

He'd left the curtains open, and outside, the moon rose full and gleaming above the trees, painting all the branches with silver.

It was a fine night. A perfect night. And when he heard the geggle-gaggle calls from a skein of geese, flying over towards the estuary, it seemed to him like it was an omen, and Robbie's heart beat all the faster.

He heard the clock in the lobby strike half past nine, then ten . . .

Nearly an hour later, he heard his mother give the fire its final poke for the night, and a short time later, the door of her room gave a click.

Then silence!

The clock struck eleven-thirty – and Robbie swung out of bed. He put his clothes on over the top of his pyjamas, carried his boots in his hand, eased up the window and was out!

He paused for a moment or two as he tied his laces, listening at the window, but there was no sound from within. Robbie crept into the wash-house, felt for the bucket in the black, found it and was off!

He'd done it!

The sky was scattered with stars and the light from the moon bathed the whole countryside in silver as Robbie ran along the track that led to the Den.

His shadow jiggled like a puppet before him, dancing merrily over the ground.

It seemed as if the whole world was asleep, and when he

stopped to rest and change the bucket to his other hand, Robbie heard no sound other than the rush of his own breathing.

The Den Wood lay before him in the hollow like a sleeping dog, growing steadily larger as he loped towards it.

And then he was there!

Robbie cupped his hands to his lips and blew into the gap between his thumbs. His owl-hoot signal carried far into the silent wood, then again.

A few seconds later, an answering hoot came clear, and then McPhee himself was stepping out of the shadows. Under an arm, he carried two sticks.

'All right?' asked McPhee quietly.

'Aye,' Robbie whispered back. 'And yourself?'

'They never heard a thing,' grinned McPhee. 'Come on, let's get going! I've brought a couple of sticks – here's hoping we need them!'

The two boys hurried, crouched low, down the length of the field, keeping close to the line of the hawthorn hedging that ran almost all the way to the riverside.

It seemed as if they could see for miles in the strange light, and soon they could see the outline of their hide down by the reeds.

As they neared it, Robbie suddenly stopped, holding McPhee by the arm.

'Look!' he breathed. 'In the field! Dozens of them!'

McPhee followed the line of Robbie's jabbing finger and there, in the stubble, between the hide and the edge of the rushes, were the plump shapes of a whole flock of greylag geese! Robbie bit at his lip in excitement!

Almost crawling now, the two boys reached the cover of a line of reeds. They eased their way along, moving the pail a foot or so in front, then wriggling forward. Easing and wriggling . . . easing and wriggling . . .

They were only a few yards away from the safety of their hide now.

Silently, hardly daring to breathe, they stole forward, keeping the hide between themselves and the geese.

And suddenly, they were there!

The two boys squeezed in together, nudging and poking each other in silent delight at their triumph.

McPhee bent back some of the grass from the hide. Robbie dipped into the pail and took out a handful of the mixture. The whisky had soaked right into the crushed oats and its pungent smell filled the hide.

Carefully, so carefully, he tossed a little out onto the stubble before them. Then again. And then some more. If the geese saw the movement, they'd be off and the whole plan ruined! Each handful was a risk they hardly dared take, but luck held, and soon Robbie had emptied the bucket and all the mixture lay in the stubble just a few feet in front of the hide!

The two boys crouched at their peepholes and the long wait began . . .

Outside, the geese cackled softly to each other, some resting with their heads tucked in below their wings, some on guard around the edges of the flocks, and some feeding in the stubble.

But as yet, none fed on the mixture!

It was cold now, and Robbie's legs began to ache.

Although the sky was clear, there was no frost, but the dampness on the ground seemed to seep right into him.

McPhee nudged him on the arm.

'Here!' he whispered in the darkness of the hide, and he fed one of the sticks into Robbie's grip.

Robbie returned to the peephole.

Some of the geese seemed closer, moving around, foraging in the stubble for food.

One came very near, waddling past less than four feet from them and Robbie saw a quick glint of the moon in its eye, and could make out the lighter colour of its feet and its bill. It didn't eat the oats, didn't even see the stuff, it seemed.

But it was followed by another bird, and this one did see the grain. The goose dipped its head down into the stubble before them and the boys could hear its bill clacking as it tasted the food.

Then again, and this time, it made pleased little noises in

91

its throat as it stretched its neck upwards and ate. Its pleasure was sensed by another goose, and soon, four of them were round the mixture, scooping it up into their bills.

Robbie gripped his fingers into McPhee's arm. McPhee was tense, scarcely breathing.

And still the geese guzzled into the oats, shovelling their bills into it, and it seemed to the two boys that there was a sort of unruliness creeping in.

The birds seemed to be well taken with the stuff.

Was it working? Was it the whisky that was making them greedy, almost reckless to get more? What if they rushed them now?

The questions raced as fast as their pulses.

But no – best to wait . . . give them time . . . let them eat more . . . let them eat the lot!

The two boys watched, dry-mouthed, at their peepholes.

The four geese were almost squabbling with each other, ruffling out their wings, barging at each other, craning their long necks forward, snapping for the food.

It was near time . . .

McPhee tugged at Robbie's sleeve, and silently, stealthily, they crept out of the gap at the rear of the hide.

Robbie felt the stick heavy in his hand as they inched round.

Slowly . . . slowly . . . slowly . . .

And then, together, they pounced!

Robbie and McPhee launched themselves forward!

In an instant, the night was filled with alarm calls as scores of wings thrashed the air, pushing, pushing, pushing away from the sudden danger!

Robbie dived to the ground!

Whether it was the whisky, or whether it was the sudden fright that froze it, Robbie never knew – but just as he hit the stubble, his hand fell across a goose's neck! His fingers clasped it instantly!

Robbie felt it come alive in his grip and struggle, and the wings clattered and crashed in panic, cracking him about the head.

But he didn't let go!

His fingers were clamped around the thick neck and were there to stay! Then he swung the stick and felt it thud onto the goose's back, stunning it. And again . . . and again . . .

With both hands now, Robbie gave a quick jerk, pulling at the bird's neck. He felt it give.

The goose fluttered and flapped on its back, but its life was already gone.

As he rose to his feet in triumph, Robbie saw McPhee thrash out at another bird, and it too was taken.

All around them, geese cackled into the night, flickering like witches across the face of the moon.

But two would never rise again.

Robbie and McPhee sent yells of delight into the air around them.

All the way home, Robbie thrilled to the weight of the dead goose in his hand. It was huge and fat and heavy, and with every step, the boy could feel the excitement rush up in him. He'd got a goose, a real live goose – at least, it had been!

He chuckled to himself as he imagined his mother's face in the morning. The best thing would be to put it on the kitchen table for her to find first thing!

Then he could help her pluck it, and singe off the fine feathers that they missed, and prepare it and cook it and carve it . . . his mouth fair watered at the thought!

Robbie coaxed up his window and swung quietly inside, dragging the weight of the goose in after him. He took off his boots and tip-toed through to the kitchen, trailing the great dead bird behind him.

He pushed open the door, and as it swung wide, he saw that the room was bright with light.

Robbie blinked, and saw before him his mother, her arms folded, her face clouded, her foot tapping in time to her temper!

Behind her, was the large, forbidding figure of Sergeant Baxter – the Local Police Force himself!

For what seemed an age, no one moved and no one spoke.

The boy with the dead goose stared up at the woman and the policeman – and the woman and the policeman stared down at the boy with the dead goose!

And then the silence was shattered by Robbie's mother!

'Just what have you been up to?' she shrieked. 'You've had me worried sick! I woke up, went through to your room to make sure you were tucked in and – and nothing!'

Her voice rose and rose until it could rise no more! She paused for breath and started all over again!

'Worried sick, I was! I – I've even been up to the phone-box and poor Sergeant Baxter's come pedalling all the way up here on his bike!'

Robbie swallowed hard, then held out the goose. Its head lay drooped over his arm, and spots of blood dripped like sealing wax from its bill onto the floor.

'Goose?' howled his mother. 'I'll give you goose, my lad!'

She lunged forward to grab the boy, but Robbie side-stepped and his mother was left clutching the dead bird by the throat! With a yowl, she dropped it to the floor!

Robbie made to jink past her, but she whipped round and caught him by the ear.

Sergeant Baxter cleared his throat and tucked his note-book back into the top pocket of his tunic.

'Ah well, now,' he said to Robbie's mother. 'I see you have the matter well in hand. I'll just be getting down the road again . . .'

He buttoned the top button of his uniform, and cleared his throat again. Then he wiped at his mouth with his hand.

'Aye,' he said, smacking his lips. 'It's a right cold night, is it not . . . ?'

Robbie's mother relaxed her grip on the boy's ear and turned to the policeman.

'Oh, Sergeant Baxter,' she said. 'How thoughtless of me. Would you – would you care for a wee dram to warm you up on the journey?'

The sergeant pretended to be surprised at the offer.

'Oh, how kind you are,' he smiled, licking at his lips again.

94

'Well now, a wee dram sounds like a grand idea . . .'

Robbie, already in fear of the hiding that was sure to come, looked on like a doomed rabbit.

His mother reached into the press for the whisky bottle, uncorked it, and poured a large measure into a glass.

'Your very good health!' declared Sergeant Baxter grandly.

And he tipped the lot down his throat.

Robbie closed his eyes.

FAREWELLS

AT THE END of the potato harvest, when the crop was all
lifted and stored under thick, dry straw in the long shed, the
tinks packed up and left their camp in the hollow of the Den
Wood.

They moved inland for the winter, to find whatever labouring
work they could to see them through to springtime.

Robbie and McPhee stood silent at the top of the Den on
the night before they were leaving.

For long hours, they listened to the owls hoot, and watched
the moon move above them in the heavens – and below them
in the looking-glass waters of the quarry-hole.

And when they talked, it was to remember the fun and the
laughter they'd had – and would have again when the year
turned once more.

Then late on, when it was time for parting, they both
hacked at the ground with their heels to dig up a stone each.
They spat on them for luck, and flung them far out.

The stones landed together on the silver moon, shattering
it into a thousand fragments.

It was still dancing on the rippling water when Robbie
reached the rise at the top of the road that led from the Den.

He turned and walked backwards, waving to the tiny figure
that waved to him in the silver light.

And even when they could no longer see each other, the two
boys still waved . . .